Contents

Once upon a time...

...in Gilesgate, a spark of an idea came to life.

Books are fun. A good story always stirs something inside of us. Children of all abilities are capable of the most fantastic creations when given time and freedom to imagine.

In a world of SATs, league tables and electronic distractions maybe people on all sides need reminding that story-telling is fun, and important.

This idea starts, as so many stories start, with a thought:

"I wonder if..."

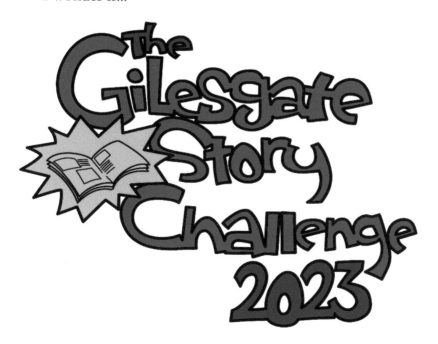

Foreword

By Simon Berry

Welcome to our new book! This is our fourth book, and we're quite proud of it.

For those of you who don't know about our project, the Gilesgate Story Challenge is a short story competition aimed at our local schools. Each year we run the competition using a different theme and donate all the proceeds to a different local charity.

This year we asked our authors to write stories with a unexpected ending.

Our competition is all about the fun of telling stories and we aim to be as all inclusive as possible. We don't alter grammar, or change the phrasing. Some of the stories may be slightly difficult to read in parts but you are genuinely reading the authors voice.

You are about to read some fantastic stories. Our patients and the children of the North East are amazingly talented and this story competition just demonstrates the breadth of that talent and imagination.

We've got everything within these pages: thrillers; mysteries; spy stories; sci-fi; fantasy and so much more. They are sometimes scary, often hilarious and always original.

I think our mix of stories is so unique this year because a lot of our authors view and interpret the world in a slightly different way. There are many stories written in an unconventional way, and with a plot that develops different to the norm. I think they capture that sideways look at the world, a unique way of telling a story, and it has made such a positive difference to our book.

I'm very proud of all of the children that have been inspired enough to enter this competition and I hope they are equally proud to see their work in print.

I'm also really grateful for the work of the teachers involved in the various schools that helped inspire children to enter their stories. Some teachers have inspired so much that they even feature in the story! Our winning story

HANNAH features the author's English teacher as one of their main characters. (I haven't been able to find out yet whether everyone in the school is really scared of her or not!)

Thank you too to our celebrity judges Lisette Auton and Kylie Dixon. Both are hugely talented children's authors and if you haven't read their books you should really look them up. A big thank you also to our regular volunteers, the amazing people that make the Gilesgate Story Challenge happen - Miles Nelson and Esther Robson.

We always illustrate the winning entry and our guest illustrator this year is Dr. Sam Strong. She is multitalented lecturer from Aston University. It's great to have Sam involved and I'm so grateful she agreed to bring HANNAH to life.

We are also lucky this year to again have some amazing illustrations from students at New College Durham. They have supplied illustrations for the short listed stories. Thank you to Clare Dickenson for again organising and inspiring our illustrators.

I'm not going to waffle this year because you need to get on with reading these amazing stories, but just in case you've noticed a bit of extra colour around….

We never have an entry fee for our competition, but this year we asked our authors to sprinkle some wildflower seeds on patches of rough ground as part of their entry 'fee.' The idea is that as our book was being published, patches of wildflowers would start to spring up in surprising places. We would create unexpected bursts of colour around the city to go with our surprising endings.

So if you are walking around the town and see those bursts of unexpected colour and it makes you smile… you might have one of our authors to thank for that!

Enjoy the stories.

Winning Entries

First Place
H.A.N.N.A.H

Story By Callum Gudge

The average day at Barbara Pristman is… interesting to say to least.

Especially English, I moved up to GCSE English and it was different, everybody seemed scared of the teacher!

At first I don't know why everybody is scared of the English teacher but it only took a week understand.

Tuesday:

The normal English teacher wasn't in so we were listening to the substitute read so that was pretty chill.

Wednesday:

The same thing happened, she wasn't in again so we did the same thing.

Thursday:

The game is now afoot, I was a bit confused because she came in with a big trolley with lots of pens and pencils, lots of them especially green and blue, and she seems quite nice I thought.

Apparently she pokes students in the eye…

…And has a 'chokey'…

…but of course I thought it was all make believe but I would find out in the wrong place and the wrong time.

I can't remember what we did on my first day but I remember getting green pen (this would be everyday with Hannah).

It wasn't bad, in fact I found it to be a lot more encouraging then my old English class.

Friday:

It is a Friday and that means only one thing…
SPELLINGS (I hate them) I can't spell even if my life
depended on it, but spellings with Hannah is actual torture,
both teachers did the same thing but I just couldn't spell
for the life of me, I got 1/10

Ouf
Beb
PneumonoultramicroscopicsilicovolcanoKoniosis
To

Yes I am a disappointment, the spelling were:

- Cat
- Dog
- Yes

- No
- On
- Off
- Bed
- Pneumonoultramicroscopicsilicovolcanokoniosis
- Two
- Tree

Just try and guess which one I got right!

Anyways… It was an absolute nightmare!

Finishing spellings was like a breath of fresh air, I left English fed up and defeated.

The Weekend →

The Weekend:

I have a weekly routine on weekends, going to my dad's house, playing football and chilling.

My time at my dad's is short so I have to get the most out of it, sometimes I blink and a hour had passed, that's how short it feels.

Monday:

It's the start of the week and I HATE the start of a week (because I'm tired) On Monday we do question of the week, it's just a question we need to answer (pretty boring)

Monday in English is ok but it's so slow, 10 minutes feel like 10 months, but it's not a bad day.

Tuesday:

Tuesday is pretty much the same, random plan and lots of writing, I like writing personally but I know some people don't.

Wednesday:

this is where it hit me, my friend bobby was missing, it was strange because throughout his life, he had never missed a day at school. I was questioning all the teachers asking "have you seen bobby? All the teachers said "no" or "he's probably sick" I knew that wasn't the case as the kid has an immune system made out of bricks.

But then I went to English. Hannah was acting very strange, all the kids were saying "he's probably in the chokey" I replied with a short and sweet "shut up".

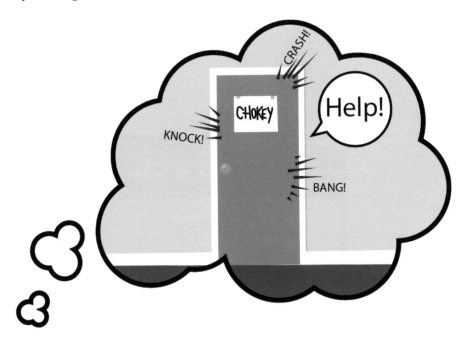

but then I mentioned bobby to Hannah and she quickly changed the topic.

"Nice weather today, isn't it?" I was confused, she quickly walked away and my brain started fearing the worst.

Thursday:

Bobby still wasn't in! I knew something was up and I would only find out by doing some digging. my mum was saying "he's probably sick Callum" but my brain was saying Hannah's done something to bobby, the day was slow and boring, but I waited until 9pm to do the imaginable, I was going to break into the school, Bobby is my friend and I do my best to find my buddy.

9pm :

I put on a full black tracksuit and a black face mask, I walked the full hour from my house to the school. When I got the school I hopped over the fence and got up to the main entrance, to my surprise it opened and I was in, but the school has doors that require special badges to open, but I had a plan, one of my teachers left their badges at school.

I had taken it, I know if I was caught I would get in serious trouble, but I was willing to go the distance, I went through the doors with ease then went straight to Hannah's English room.

I found a receipt which had £1000 worth of green and blue pen, It was pretty strange but I was getting off track, I need to find out what happened to Bobby, there was this big white door which was a huge key hole, the handle was also huge, with hesitation I opened the door

…and saw Bobby with Hannah, doing English work.

I was very confused and found this whole situation weird, I asked "what's going on here? Bobby seemed happy to see me "Callum! What a nice surprise, I was just catching up on some English work."

I asked "Why haven't you been in school for the last two days?"

He replied "I have, I've been in here cleaning this room out" I left with lots of questions and concerns, I guess Hannah's not evil after all.

THE END

Second Place

Story By Ben Bradley

Check page 161 for illustrator credits!

One day, there was an ordinary guy whose name was Christopher. He stepped inside the kitchen where food and dinner is prepared for him. He finds the lucky tin of biscuits and he decides to consume one. It was one delicious biscuit, but right when he was about to leave the weird kitchen, his father stops him! "Don't eat any more of those deadly biscuits. They are too dangerous for humans." he shouted angrily. He told his son all about the story of how the biscuits were created by an evil businessman guy who puts sharp and pointy things in food, like nails and knives.

Christopher was so terrified that he decided to not eat biscuits for an entire week. He was getting drastically slower and weaker each day. It turns out that the biscuits, which his father said were an evil treat, are the source of Christopher's energy and power. Now that he hadn't eaten any for days, he became too weak that he couldn't be able to breathe anymore!

His strange father was laughing like an insane person as he watched his son struggle to survive each second. "Oh, my dear son. You thought I was a human this entire time. But it turns out I'm really an alien from outer space!" he shouted maniacally.

His skin started turning green, like an alien and had such scary, abnormal eyes that don't look like it belongs to this planet at all. The alien brought out his frightening laser gun, but suddenly, a random cowboy person broke into the house through the window.

The brave cowboy told the alien to stop his evilness but the alien hopped into his UFO, (an unidentified flying object) and shot a million lasers at the cowboy.

"Nice try, but my trusty cowboy hat makes me invincible!" the powerful cowboy laughed frantically. The lasers bounced off his hat and back at the alien's UFO. His flying spaceship exploded in seconds!

Without his UFO, the alien was defeated. The cowboy grabbed his scary cowboy gun and shot the alien until he died. They never heard from that other planet being ever again.

The powerful cowboy found the weak and slow Christopher. "Here, have some biscuits, son. They are your source of power." he said as he fed the little boy thousands of tasty biscuits.

Suddenly, Christopher felt strong and fast again. He was amazed. "How did you know that biscuits were my source of power?" Christopher questioned, still very shocked of the alien's defeat. The cowboy showed Chris his shiny golden badge. Christopher recognised that badge. He had a flashback of when he was only two years old. He remembered his father having a shiny golden badge, just like the cowboy's. Christopher suddenly realised what it meant. He gasped with surprise.

The cowboy is his real father! "Where have you been this entire time?" confused Christopher asked.

"I've known about the aliens invading for years. The aliens captured me and put me in their prison for a long time! One of the aliens impersonated me and tricked you into thinking he was your father. Luckily, I escaped."

Christopher was proud of his father's awesome quest. But, this was surely not the end of the invasion of aliens. Surely they'll come back with an alien army to attack Earth! But, that's in the future and we don't need to worry about that!

"Dad, let's order Domino's pizza for the celebration." Chris cheered with joy and happiness of being proud to be his father's son. Later, in the evening, Christopher's father went to Domino's to collect the pizza, but what he didn't know is that there were evil Martians waiting to capture him. This was a trap planned for him. The doors locked. Unfortunately, Chris's father, Carl the cowboy, got captured by the malicious aliens once again.

Will he escape this time? No one knows…

Joint Third
An Unexpected Visitor

Story By Niamh Poppleton
Check page 161 for illustrator credits!

Foreseen many centuries ago was the coming of the visitors: creatures of the darkness who bask under the moonlight. What they would look like, nobody knew. When they would come was even more unclear. Yet, the fact still remained that someday they would arrive, and when they did they would be searching. Written down on paper were the prophecies foretold by the witches that once roamed the plains. After years upon years of waiting, the concept itself turned to myth. Nobody thought they would come; nobody thought it would be them who the visitors searched for.

On a Hallows Eve night, as the wind whisked ferociously through the stormy grey skies above and the moon settled full between the speckles of light we call stars, nobody suspected a thing. Not even as they plummeted down from whatever ungodly world they fell from and cried like a new-born child – not even as they crawled from the ground and drew nearer and nearer to the town.

Everything was as normal as normal can be in a town with a history of witchcraft and wonder that at night still haunted the air. Whispers of the dead called out their truths, tapping against the panes of glass that withheld the outside world from the residents, though it was merely rain before the storm. Tap. Tap. Tap. Droplets clung to the windows.

Sitting within a house, with the orangey glow of a small candle lighting the room, was a girl. Her hair cascaded down her shoulders and back, black and thin like feathers of a raven, as she turned the crinkled old pages of a leather-bound book. The ghost of a smile flitted across her face as her eyes scanned the words that darted from Latin to Greek, whispering the incantations beneath her breath, her fingers tracing the words as she spoke.

A flash of light dashed past the window – sparks of white and gold flickering through the darkness, followed by a crashing sound that filled the air like fog over the mountaintops. Even so, the girl continued reading, whispering, as the ball of black fluff that she had named Destiny, an animal that she fed and watched over but did not own, stared at the door with curious eyes, meowing softly.

Tap. Tap. Tap. Sounds of the rain pouring from the heavens above were not dying down, as they fell more viciously, hitting against the windows more hurriedly. Though the next tapping noise that came was more like a rapping: a knocking of skin upon wood, nothing like water grasping on to glass. It was coming from the door. A thick, persistent knocking to the beat of a heart.

Dudum.

Dudum.

Whatever it was, was calling the girl – her name was intertwined between the knocks. Almost trancelike she arose, gracefully tiptoeing across the room, a haze over her eyes as though she had been cursed in fog and storm. Her bony fingers stumbled as she unlatched the lock at the top of the door and she heaved as she pulled on the icy, metallic handle – for some reason, it seemed almost heavier than usual, as though the metal itself was warning her not to open the door.

There stood the visitor – lanky and emaciated and knowing, in the doorway. Its fingers were spindly; its body draped in a gown of black; an orangey red glow looming around it's figure as though it had taken the essence of hell and bathed in it. As it glanced upwards, staring the girl down, with embers of fire dancing within its eyes, she found herself with only one question: why does its face look like mine?

Silence.

Never seen again. That is all that is said and heard about the girl. Except, in this circumstance 'never' is contingent upon what people perceive, and when one person sees her roaming the plains once more, that can no longer be the case. I suppose that the girl will be seen again… Perhaps – if the prophecies are true – the visitors will be too.

An Unexpected Visitor

A Comic by Elliot Conway
Story by Niamh Poppleton

Foreseen many
centuries ago
was the
coming of the
visitors:
creatures of
the darkness
who bask
under the
moonlight.

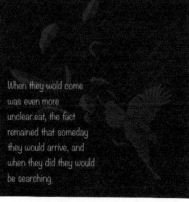

When they wold come
was even more
unclear.eat, the fact
remained that someday
they would arrive, and
when they did they would
be searching

What they
would look like,
nobody knew

On a hallows eve
night, as the wind
whisked
ferociously
through the
stormy grey skies
above and the
moon settled full
between the
speckles of light
we call stars

Written down on paper were the prophecies foretold by the
witches that once roamed the plains
After years upon years of waiting, the concept itself
turned to myth.
Nobody thought they would come: nobody thought it would be
them who the visitors searched for.

Nobody suspected
a thing

Not even as they plummeted down
from whatever ungodly world they
fell from and cried like a new-
born child – not even as they
crawled from the ground and
drew nearer and nearer to the
town.

Whispers of the dead called out their truths, tapping against the panes of glass that withheld the outside world from the residents.

Everything was as normal as normal can be in a town with a history of witchcraft and wonder that at night till haunted the air

Though it was merely rain before the storm.

TAP TAP TAP

Droplets clung to the windows.

Sitting within a house, with orangey glow of a small candle lighting the room, was a girl. Her hair cascaded down her shoulders and back, black and thin like feathers of a raven, as she turned the crinkled old pages of a leather-bound book.

The ghost of a smile flitted across her face as her eyes scanned the words that darted from Latin to Greek, whispering the incantations beneath her breathe, her fingers tracing the words as she spoke.

A flash of light dashed past the window – sparks of white and gold flickering through the darkness, followed by a cashing sound that filled the air like fog over the mountaintops.

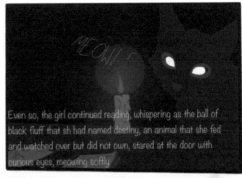

Even so, the girl continued reading, whispering as the ball of black fluff that sh had named destiny, an animal that she fed and watched over but did not own, stared at the door with curious eyes, meowing softly

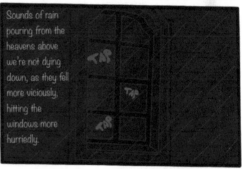

Sounds of rain pouring from the heavens above we're not dying down, as they fell more viciously, hitting the windows more hurriedly.

Though the next tapping noise that came was more like a rapping; a knocking of skin upon wood, nothing like water grasping on to glass.

It was coming from the door

A thick, persistent knocking to the beat of a heart

Dadum

Whatever it was, was calling the girl — her name intertwined between the knocks.

Dadum

Dadum

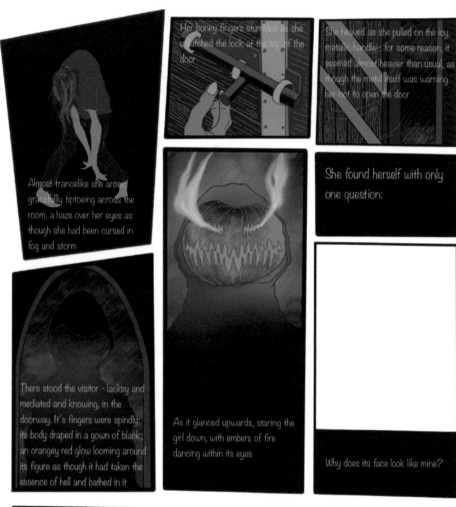

Her boney fingers stumbled as she unlatched the lock at the top of the door

She heaved as she pulled on the icy, metallic handle - for some reason, it seemed almost heavier than usual, as though the metal itself was warning her not to open the door

Almost trancelike she arose, gracefullly tiptoeing across the room, a haze over her eyes as though she had been cursed in fog and storm

She found herself with only one question:

There stood the visitor - lackey and mediated and knowing, in the doorway. It's fingers were spindly; its body draped in a gown of black; an orangey red glow looming around its figure as though it had taken the essence of hell and bathed in it

As it glanced upwards, staring the girl down, with embers of fire dancing within its eyes

Why does its face look like mine?

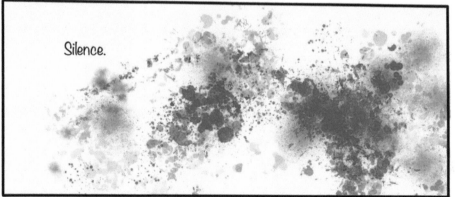

Silence.

Never seen again. That is all that is said
and heard about the girl. Except, in this
circumstance "never" is contingent upon
what people perceive, an when one person
sees her roaming the plains once more, that
can no longer be the case. I suppose that
the girl will be seen again... perhaps - if the
prophecies are true - the visitors will be too.

Joint Third

The Mystery of Goldsmith Mansion

Story By Wendy Ransom
Check page 161 for illustrator credits!

Inspector Bella Smith was concerned.

She was not only concerned for the Goldsmith's family diamond (also named "The Great Gold Diamond ", as it was famous for its size) but also the terrible history of the Goldsmith Mansion, where the gem was housed before it got stolen.

She had been rudely awoken at 3 am this morning due to a break in at the Goldsmith's family home. On further inspection, the theft of the diamond was confirmed and an emergency was declared. Bella had put some research into the house and learned of its unfortunate past.

In 1864, A. Ruby (a maid) was murdered with no method of death confirmed.

In 1902, part of the original house burnt down, along with half of the family fortune.

Just last year, residents made a huge statement in the press, claiming they were being haunted and hearing sounds in the night. This is yet to be confirmed as a myth.

The gem, on the other hand, was confirmed in the house at 11:00 pm, so it must have been stolen from 11:00 to 3:00. Inspector Smith had at least 12 theories in her head by the time she had got to the house. When she got there, there were forensic investigators everywhere (testing for fingerprints, no doubt) and her investigator friends were already interviewing the residents.

As soon as she saw the house, it sent a shiver down her spine. It really did look as though a murder could happen and nobody would turn a head. Nevertheless, she had a mystery to solve, and any clue was a lead in this crime. She entered the house, completely ignoring the "POLICE LINE:DO NOT CROSS" tape strung across the entire house.

Honestly, police these days went over the top on these things.

She passed straight past everyone else and into the vault room. She pulled a state-of-the-art fingerprint scanner out and she scanned the pedestal that the diamond used to stand. It came up with 2 matches: The Lady of the House, Lady A Goldsmith and Mr Stockman, the butler. She guessed that one was a cleaner; the other was a thief.

She quietly strode out the room and went to read the interview papers. She saw that Mr Stockman had been cleaning that evening, which was certainly suspicious because he hadn't been in his room. On the other hand, Lady Goldsmith had refused to give anything but "I was asleep." Bella thought this was also rather suspicious. She went into the house to look for more clues.

Police bustled around the place, swarmed by reporters from many different sources. She also privately thought that reporters shouldn't be allowed into places where detectives were at work. They could mess with something and end up getting arrested for something they didn't do.

She held some papers in her hand. They were the interviews for all the other people in the household at the time. They all stated that they knew where all others were at the time, including Lady Goldsmith and Mr Stockman. She found Lord Goldmans room and began to open the drawers with some plastic gloves on.

Wait! Gloves! That's it!

The culprit could have been wearing gloves. She frantically started searching drawers for gloves, or even the diamond itself. None in the Lord's room. None in the Butler's room. Not even any in the Lady's room. Last room.

Amanda Goldsmith, Lady Goldsmith's daughter. She searched every single draw, even unlocking an old oak jewelry box. Nothing. A thought came to her. Last year, there was an unsolved case after a museum's ruby went missing. The ruby was found taped underneath a drawer in an empty apartment near the museum. She pulled all the drawers out and checked the bottoms.

On the last one, there was an envelope taped underneath. With a smirk, she carefully ripped it open. Inside there was a pair of ladies gloves, one with a large diamond inside. In only a few hours, Bella had solved a case which remains unsolved today.

Because Bella Smith died 20 years ago after the missing ruby case. She was the best inspector the police have had in 100 years.

The police have missed her dearly and unknown to them she has solved every case since!

The End

Judges' Favourites

Simon's Favourite

Story By Alex Potts
Check page 161 for illustrator credits!

One time there was a couple they lived a normal life in a normal house. The lady was called Karen, her husband was called Kevin, and they were both vegans. Kevin was in hospital for a long time because Karen pushed him down the stairs for asking what meat tastes like. Once Kevin recovered from hospital Kevin decided to divorce. Karen was very upset but she understood what had to be done. So she went to search for a new husband particularly one who was vegan.

She asked every man that she saw if he was vegan but then after 3 months and 12 nights at different hotels she came across a man who seemed to have an interest in her and… Karen had an interest in him! She ran up to him and asked if he was vegan. He hesitated at first and he replied with "yes and my name is Chris" but Karen jumped to things to quickly and asked if Chris wanted to marry her. "Let's just get to know each other first" Chris replied, Karen agreed and before you know it they started dating. Karen finally felt like she had another shot at love.

They got a taxi back home and had dinner. When they sat down at the table and Chris asked where the pork was. Karen burst out laughing. "Funny joke" she said Chris replied with "hilarious I know" 5 days later Karen went to go to work but, before she left Chris told her that he wasn't feeling well so Karen gave him a hug and left. Karen worked as a cashier so when people had meat in their bag she would glare at them even children would get the glare. When she arrived back home it was pitch black so she turned on all the lights and went to look for Chris. She looked up stairs he wasn't there then she searched downstairs he wasn't there. She was about to give up but then she saw the refrigerator door wide open… Karen went over to investigate, she looked inside and found a big cardboard box inside and it said Chris's secret stash and inside was… big red meat barbeque ribs, hot dogs, peperoni, beef, pork and loads more. Karen couldn't believe her eyes she almost fainted. With pure rage she remembered the only place she didn't check his car… she stormed outside and went to his car. She opened his car door only to find Chris devouring meat, before he could say anything. She stole his car keys and locked him in the car. She went inside and then came out with a lighter came over to the car opened the fuel tank in the car and set it on fire! BOOM! The car blew up and his burned body landed in a nearby tree. 1 minute later the police arrived and pulled up in front of Karen and arrested her.

47

She later woke up in prison, a guard was taking her picture and he said you have been arrested for murder, vandalism and tax fraud. Karen was very sad. Over the years she was known as the big boss of prison because at lunch time she would slap anyone who had meat. And whenever someone stood up to her they would fall.

10 years later… Karen was released from jail and went home to watch TV, she saw on the news that the president received the biggest pack of ribs from a famous chef. This made Karen mad so she went to try to kill the president. To be continued…

(This story is not supposed to offend anyone, just a joke!)

-Alex Potts

Miles' Favourite

The Laboratory

Story By Hope Nicholl

Check page 161 for illustrator credits!

In a laboratory underground an explosion happened.

"Well done 007 you may head back now," a rough voice said to the girl.

A girl with emerald green skin and ocean blue eyes and hair walked down with a plain white outfit. She walked in a room filled with white pillows to her close friend.

"How was it?" her friend asked in a sweet voice.

"Good Adder, can't wait for the next one," 007's voice panted in response.

"Nice. So what power level do you have?" Adder asked.

"I think a level 5. But what lesson do you have next? I have target practise." 007 said responding to Adder's question.

"So the same as last time. I have the power check-up." Adder said.

A bash told Adder to head to the power check-up. So Adder with her scales, red skin, blood red hair and golden green eyes, her tail was flickering heading to the main hall. When Adder came to the main hall test dummies were in place and Adder sliced them to bits with her tail splattered them in oil. She then went to her venom test and bit into the target, it showed that she was the strongest snake human hybrid in the school!

"Nice one. Meet me out side for a scale absorption test." A mysterious voice asked Adder.

As Adder went out for her scale absorption test she met a new student.

"Hey are you new here?" Adder asked with a sweet but disturbing voice to the rattle snake who was coloured black and white with sand-coloured eyes and tail.

"Yeah, Viper is the name. Heading to the scale absorption test, first one. But why did they steal us from our homes?" Viper asked with her fangs showing and tail rattling.

"It's because we are too dangerous for the outside world. Oh and adders the name. Come now all humanoid snakes hybrids head to the scale absorption test," Adder responded.

Viper nodded as they half walked and slithered to the outside dome. They laid down with the other humanoid snake hybrids. Some were on branches others were on rocks. The sea snakes had their own little area. Adder and Viper went on a branch.

A beam of light shone down and all the human snakes relaxed but Viper, who was a sea and land snake hybrid so she was a triple hybrid. Viper went to the mud and it was better, the mud was softer against her scales. The scientists were confused and when the test was over they tested Vipers blood and found out what she was but still treated her the same.

"Hey Adder. I have something to tell you," Viper said, wrapping her rattle snake striped tail around Adders tail.

"What is it Viper?" Adder asked curiously. "Oh and this is my roommate 007 or Seven for short," as she introduced Seven.

"Nice to meet you Viper," Seven went in for a hand shake but viper refused because she doesn't trust her yet.

"Nice to meet, Seven. But anyways, I am sea snake, human and land snake hybrid can you believe it." Viper said happily.

"That's amazing!" Adder congrats Viper. "Well done viper. Say what is your power or powers?" Seven ask gently.

"Well I can: Breathe underwater and on land, stronger venom and I can't remember anything else," Viper confessed smirking.

The end...

The Laboratory

A comic by Izzy Reed
Story by Hope Nicholl

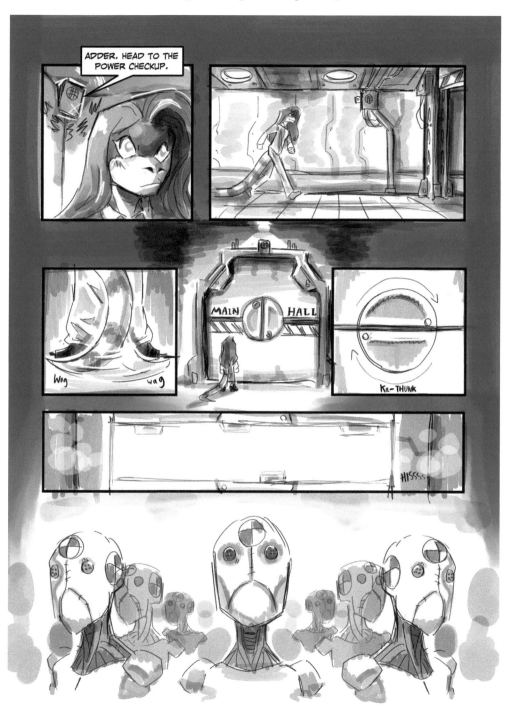

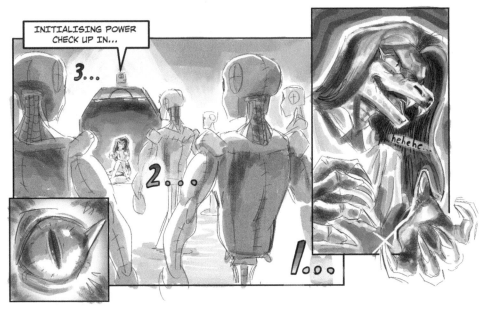

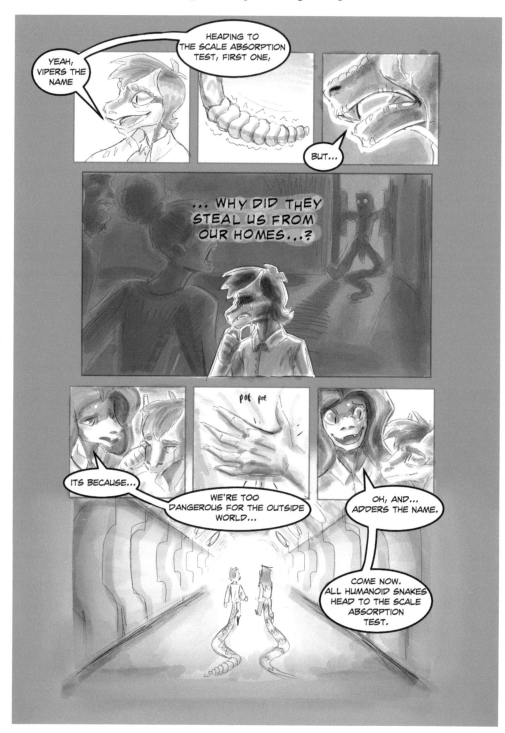

Special Mentions

Although the following stories didn't win, they still ooze with whimsy and charm.... Or sometimes even intrigue and spookiness!

The Quest

By Adam Bowman

Once there was a guy called Beau he was kind, caring and handsome. He lived in a house with his mam, dad and sister. One day he was playing in a grassy field with his friends, when a wizard approached him and said "you have to go on a quest to save the world. An evil person has got his hands on a very powerful rock."

Beau was amazed but he wondered why was he chosen? So that night he told his family they were astonished to and they said that he could go. So the next day he packed his things and set off, with his two friends Patrick and Finn.

Once they were out of town Beau pulled out a map "we are going to the volcano." Beau explained. Finn told the others that he'd saw something in the trees! Patrick was scared, Finn comforted him.

Then they saw it!

It was tall, scary and pale. It stepped out of the darkness. It said "Hi I'm Sophie." She told the boys her story, she was an outcast from her town because of her scars (She had a huge scar on her face). The boys said "That was a good story."

They asked if Sophie wanted to join them on their quest. Sophie agreed.

As they were walking, they found an old, overgrown dungeon. They decided to go inside. After a while, they saw a tall young man who looked like he was lost. Patrick shouted "Hey you over there!"

The man looked over and saw them. He walked over slowly. He said "My name is Riley, I've been lost in this maze for a really long time." He took a breath. "Where are you guys going?"

Beau, Finn, Patrick and Sophie were skeptical to tell him as he seemed sketchy but they just said "somewhere."

They said to him "Would you like to come with us."

Riley yelled "YESSSS!" As he ran towards them.

They then walked into a room with a narrow hole in the ceiling. Just then Beau, Patrick and Sophie heard a loud scream they looked behind them and saw Riley with a sharp knife with blood dripping off it, next to him, on the floor they saw Patrick with blood coming out of his leg. They rushed to help him but just then the walls started to close in everyone started to panic they ran to the middle of the room. They knew what they must do, they needed to get out. Riley (who still felt bad for stabbing Patrick), said "I will sacrifice myself." The others were shocked but they did still remember what he did so Riley stretched up to the ceiling and the others climbed up on his back (Patrick limped up). Eventually everyone was at the top except Riley. Beau said "good bye." As Riley was crushed by the wall.

Now they were back on the road, they saw the volcano (which was their destination). As they were walking towards the volcano, a fire troll ran at them, Patrick was terrified, Beau rummaged through his bag but the only thing he could find was a… Orange! He held it in his hand and squeezed it the juice went everywhere and into the troll's eyes as it fell back into the gushing river below. They were happy as they defeated it. They plodded on up the volcano, being careful not to fall. After sometime, they reached the top and met… mark (the bad guy). He said "I've been expecting you."

Patrick trembled with fear but beau was ready. He ran towards mark as mark ran towards him, beau shouted "I'm here for the powerful rock!"

Mark shouted in reply "Well you're not getting it!"

Beau pulled out his sword and so did mark, Beau had managed to get mark on the edge of the lava but he wasn't strong enough and fell in. Mark (who didn't expect to beat Beau) was shocked he laughed and celebrated. But he lost his balanced and fell in.

Meanwhile, Patrick, Finn and Sophie were very sad. Two days later they arrived back in the village and went to Beau's where his family were. Finn broke the news, Beau's family were devastated. After that, the town was never the same again.

THE END.

Story By Bailey Cooper Wilkinson
Check page 161 for illustrator credits!

So you're running in the freaky, frightening forest as the thunder crackles and booms, your clothes getting drenched and soaking with water. You see it, a tall brown mansion staying silent and standing motionless in the middle of nowhere right in front of you. Your only thought is to enter as your curiosity takes over. Your entire body, your legs dragging you to imminent doom.

The door opens but its empty and pitch black, nobody seems to be occupying the settlement. You creep down the deep, dark and dusky hallway as the floorboards which seem broken or bent creek and squeak under your shivering feet. But as you look directly ahead in the darkness a figure approaches with heavy footsteps, glowing red eyes scanning you. You turn on your flashlight and there you see a tall pale, skinny and ancient man wielding a large red rusty axe. With a permanent grin showing yellow and blackened teeth.

He's getting too close so you flee. You run for your life but what was slow heavy footsteps becomes a rumbling fast charge followed by demonic cackling laughter as if the mad man was finding joy in your struggling. Fearing that he will get closer and put the axe into your back you run faster. Your heart pounding but you get struck by a bear trap he left out just for you. You're in pain. The teeth of the trap digging into your bare flesh. As you turn your head you see the man breathing and towering over you whilst licking his dry, white lips. He lifts the massive axe and spoke in a spine chilling tone he says "Time…for…the…harvest" and the axe drops so fast you wake up in shock.

It was all a dream . You're safe until you look at your bedroom door. He is standing right there staring at you and waves.

You pass out and hope it will be over by morning. You wake up and exit your bedroom. You're in the same mansion, the walls are the same, the windows too then you remember your living at your grandpa's place for the 6 weeks holidays.

Then grandpa walks in the room he stands there grinning with his golden teeth and then you realise he looks just like the man from the nightmare probably because you dreamt that your grandpa killed you with the axe he chops trees. A bit strange why you dreamt your grandpa was a psychopath axe man.

Why are you so scared of your dear….old…grandpa? He's just a friendly lumberjack who lives alone.

"ok boy" he said in a soft tone " take the axe and follow me we are chopping some trees for money and maybe we can go hunting." so you follow him outside in the nice warm weather going to the nearest tree and chopping. After a while you forget the dream calling it silly and telling yourself it's not real……..until you walk over with logs in your arms and go see grandpa. You drop all the logs in horror to see grandpa on the floor presumably dead but when you get closer he rises up with his back turned as he starts dislocating his body parts, twisting and turning, cracking and crunching and then stops. You stay silent hoping he doesn't notice you but he turns his head 150 degrees and stares right at you, his body pale brown and grey as if a zombie then he gets ya.

You manage to break free but the mad man is back and he's terrifyingly fast. You run to the mansion you don't look back even though you can feel his presence right behind you as if he were a guided missile.

You get into the house and lock the door you hear a thud. Has he ran head first into the door? But then you hear more banging, he's breaking the door down with huge blows of his axe he looks directly at you with his red eye through an opening that he made with his axe.

You run to the basement and lock the basement door, you hear heavy footsteps as you sense the man searching you. You see a box in the corner and you but its locked so you hack the lock of with your axe it's a Tommy gun and its loaded. You take it, its heavy and cold but it's useful. You creep out the basement and search your surroundings but as you look up he's right above you crawling on the ceiling like a spider. You open fire the machine gun rattling as bullets fly and shells drop but it's not killing him, he's regenerating.

You retreat and search for a while for more supplies. Then you come across a barrel full of fireworks and dynamite. You grab the fireworks and exit the basement. You set up a trap and you're the bait.

As time passes he comes back you grab the gun and shoot at the man until he gets too close. Now's your chance shoot the explosives, all you see is bright light and you can't hear anything then you pass out.

When you wake up the whole area is burnt out and damaged, somehow you survived……well what's left of you.

The Pirate Ship Adventure

By Brandon D

Once upon a time, there was a boy name Hugh. He walked down to the beach, the beach was relatively close to Hugh's house. Within an hour, he played with his beach ball, swan in the water, and even met one of his friends Daniel walk by.

But then, something unusual happened, very unusual. A ship came across and landed on the beach Hugh was playing on. Hugh didn't know what was happening. After the three pirates came out, Hugh noticed something about them. Two of them had a scar on their face, the other one had an eyepatch on their right eye. Also, they didn't happy.

Moreover, Hugh was expecting them to fight his city. What actually happened was far from what he was expecting. All three pirates shook his hand in agreement. "Do you want to join us on an amazing adventure?" Questioned one of the pirates. "Yes, I love adventures!" Hugh replied with plead. And for the rest of the year they voyaged around the world.

Or at least they thought. While returning back to Hugh's home, more pirates from the horizon sailed alongside Hugh's ship. All the sudden, a cannonball shot the other side of the ship Hugh was on. Their ship sank below the water, there was no hope.

Hugh woke up in the hospital wondering 'where am I?' After some time, he got sent home, and got a theory that the three pirates that were with him drowned.

Story of Something

By Brendan M Powell

One day a guy called Guy was walking down a road in Birmingham and spotted a car store. He went inside and looked at all the cars.

The one car he liked the most was a very small car called the Peel P50. It was red and squeaky clean, he could even see his own reflection in it. So he decided to buy it, luckily it was on sale for only £2000. The next day he decided to give it a try and went to the road and for some reason the car went 851MPH in 0.1miliseconds, I think the car had the wrong fuel … he went very fast and crashed into someone's house and the now busted Peel P50 simultaneously combusted.

After 6 minutes of being concussed, Guy notices the police are coming as it turned out everyone in that house also simultaneously combusted so Guy had killed 12 people because the house was having a party. So Guy decided to steal a nearby Porsche and drove away. There was a freezer with 18 hotdogs in the car and there is a FIM-92 Stinger which is an Infrared surface to air missile launcher.

Currently, he is in Birmingham and is going towards London with the police still on his tail, at this time Guy is going 129.621MPH. Now the police are in big scary police helicopters with massive bright lights to find him. The chase lasted for 4 hours all of the police's attempts to catch him had failed but Guy has made it to the English Channel meaning he can't go any further. But Guy's luck is getting better, on the beach he found a working Sea plane, so he hopped onto it and started the engine, he didn't know how to fly a plane but there was a manual in a little hatch in the cockpit of the aircraft.

So, he is in the air try to fly to the Netherlands so he can lose the police who were still following Guy. There are multiple problems though the aircraft only has three hours left of fuel and Guy doesn't know how to speak any other language except English, so he won't be able to ask people for help, also he can't use google translate because he phone got destroyed in the Peel P50 crash!

He still has some cash on him so he might be able to buy a new phone, but that means he will have to convert his currency into Euros which will take ages so instead he decides to fly to Norway because some of the people there speak a bit of English and he decides to fly to a higher altitude just in case he runs out of fuel.

3 Hours Later…

Guy's plane had ran out of fuel but he was not bothered because he is landed on The Nordic shore so he hopped out of his plane and started to walk towards a nearby place called Haugesund. By this time, the police have given up the search for Guy as he has went too far from the English coast!

But it turns out that Guy was actually dreaming because he woke up and he was still in his Peel P50 and he hadn't even drove off yet he must have fell asleep when he entered the car so he drives back home with no problems…

The End

David's Narrow Escape

By Albert

Once upon a time there lived a bear called David. In a few days he was going to Africa. He was really looking forward to this exciting adventure! He was working as hard as he could to pack. He had packed a toothbrush, a pair of pyjamas, a ginormous packed lunch and of course a pen knife. He had always wanted to go to Africa and now was his chance.

A few days later he was on the plane to Africa. When he got there he saw all sorts of amazing animals. He saw a gentle giraffe, a hungry crocodile and a magnificent lion. He was approaching the beach when he saw the most magnificent animal of all time. A golden eagle he started at it as it was beautiful. But what was it doing in African or was it meant to be here?

When he got to his hotel he decided to go to the beach so he got out his bucket and spade and crossed the road to the beach. When he got there he went to some wet sand and started building a ginormous sand castle. He got some funny looks because he was a very small bear building a very big sand castle. Next he climbed some cliffs it was very scary.

When he was down from the cliffs he decided to have a swim in the sea and that's when the trouble began. As he got into the sea he saw a pair of eyes looking at him from below. He thought it was just a fish but it wasn't. He swam to the buoy and back. Then he went back to the hotel. The next day it was nice and sunny so he went to the beach to have a swim. Then as soon as he got in the sea he saw a pair of eyes looking at him. He was sure it was the same pair of eyes that he saw last time. But when he swam to the buoy the eye suddenly darted up at him. He tried his best to escape but he wasn't fast enough. He swam to the edge but the current pulled him back into the sea. But just then the current changed direction. He got pulled back to the shore. He was very relieved but the adventure was not over yet.

The next day he was going to the beach again. When he got there he saw a pair of eyes looking at him again but he was so hot so he decided he would go for as swim anyway and just then he saw another golden eagle. He did not know why they kept coming or was it the same one? Suddenly the golden eagle swooped down on him as if it recognised him. It landed on a nearby rooftop then it flew and landed on his head!!! He was just about to shake it off when it spoke. It actually spoke. Well he understood it. He knew lots of languages but he didn't know which one was which. Was it just someone dressed as a golden eagle or was it real? Suddenly as quick as it appeared it disappeared. So he decided to go for a swim but then a sea monster jumped out of the sea and fell back into it with a ginormous splash! It must have been what the eyes were!

Now David was in terrible danger and he desperately wanted to escape from it so brave little David set off on his quest. When he got back to the hotel he went up to his balcony and looked out at the sea. But there wasn't any it had gone completely. It had disappeared. Had the monster drank it all? He rushed downstairs and out of the door to investigate. Then out of the shadows rose a monster. It dived after him and suddenly it grew arms and legs and sprinted after him. Then David had an idea he ran towards the monster so the monster opened its mouth. Then David ran under its legs so it tried to follow him but unluckily for the monster it was very slippy so it fell over. Then he ran back to the airport onto the magnificent gleaming plane.

THE END

All Hail the Caesar

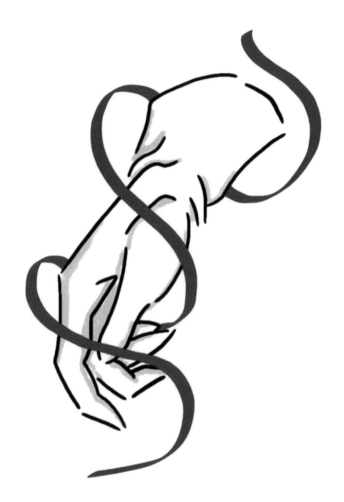

Story By Harrison L
Check page 161 for illustrator credits!

Italy: Island of Sicily

1897

The golden sun rose above the orange sky covering the surface of Sicilian soil in light causing many animals to come out from their borrows to begin their day of survival in this harsh but amazing landscape. But what made them a little different was they no longer had big predators to worry about. Unlike another group of animals living in the old town of Palermo who did have something to fear!

Gabriele Aloisio a 9 year old boy was walking down the street towards his Grandfather's old workshop, if you passed him on the street you wouldn't think anything was wrong with the poor lad, he had the same smile he always wore to bring his friends and family cheer. But, if you knew him better you could see the worry and fear in his eyes as he walked and most people knew why or assumed that it was about his Father, Venditti Aloisio the local farmer had missed his pay to the town Don Adamos so some of his boys were coming over today.

Gabriele stopped at the door to his Grandfather's wiped the tears from his eyes and opened the door putting on his brightest smile "Nonno?" he said stepping in as the sound of a hammer stopped hitting wood.

"Gabriele!" Vito Aloisio said with a smile on his face coming he picked him up carried him to his work bench. Placing him down he proceeded to ask "did you bring it?" quickly Gabriele took out his bag and gave it to his Grandfather who took it and proceeded to pull out a map from it with letters from his shelf, looking over the map he took a pen and with a smile traced down on the docks out west .

"Nonno? What are you doing?"

Vito stopped and looked at his Grandson with a joyous smile "Finding us a way out of this town boy, with this map and the money I saved we can finally get out of this hell and go anywhere!"

Gabriele gasped with surprise before standing up in joy "really! That's amazing!" he quickly stopped before looking up with sad eyes. "what about Papa?"

That caused Vito to drop his smile and sigh, he was an old man and wasn't blind at what was about to happen to his son and had spent all night grieving before he was even taken by that monster's henchmen.

Vito looked at his Grandson with determination and sadness "No Gabriele no, he has to finish work in this town but don't worry he will meet us in the New Country once we leave I promise".

Vito could see the disappointment and sadness in his eyes but also trust and hope that he was right, which broke Vito's heart even more with his lie. He didn't have time to dwell as banging on the door and voices came and Vito knew these were Adamos men.

"Boy get in the basement now!" he quickly began opening up the trap door with Gabriele scurrying in. "Don't come out until I open this door but if I take far too long...there's the back entrance."

quickly Vito closed the door just as the front one was kicked in and two men walked with rifles raised ready to kill Vito for being late. "Lower those weapons boys".

A heavy Greek accent was heard from the front with Vito's heart beat quickening in terror as Don Adamos Angelos came through with a grin.

Adamos was an intimidating man who made his own bodyguards look like little boys, with a height of 6'6 and scars from head to toe Adamos was not someone you wanted to anger or meet. "Greetings Mr Aloisio, how are you on this fine day?"

Vito said nothing and glared at him with a hatred but Adamos was unfazed. "As you most likely know Venditti missed out on his pay for the month and the last."

Vito growled and looked at him. "And you killed him"

Adamos put an understanding face and dropped his grin. "No sir instead I offered him a deal give me half of all the food he makes and I shall leave him alone".

Vito's eyes grew in surprise but then anger. "That food belongs to the people!"

Adamos grew a grin again, "so you want me to kill your son?" Vito's face dropped in sadness and shook his head. Adamos grinned even further and with a snap of his fingers in came two more men with a bag, Adamos then said "While Venditti is off the hook you still need to pay. You're due for this month."

Vito sighed and pulled out some of the money he had, "This is all I have for this month take it and get out", it was a lie of course but he couldn't let them know about his stash - not when they were so close to getting out of here.

"This will do for now but we will be back!" Adamos said bringing out a bag of his own with Vito growing worried and confused. "Listen this is from Venditti it's food for you and the boy, I wanted to give it to you personally to show I'm not fully a monster." and with that they all left with Adamos growing a grin again.

Vito quickly closed the door put the bag on the table and opening the trap door, "boy come out its safe now". Gabriele came out hugging his Grandfather with happiness, "did you hear Don Angelos Nonno? Papa is alright!"

Vito chuckled while picking him up and putting him on the table. "And he gave us food for the night!" Gabriele quickly grabbed the bag and opened it with hungry eyes before dropping it screaming.

Vito looked down and his face dropped as out came… the head of Venditti Aloisio and a note attached with - *fooled you!*

Miley's Journey

By Isabel O

It all started on a cold, damp, dark night you could have heard the blizzard blowing through the wind. But, if you listened closely you could hear the stomping of many feet through the thick, fresh snow. A group of people were slowly walking in the blizzard being weighed down by the large, bulky bags their carrying on their backs. In this group there was a mother and daughter the mothers name was Annie, she was 37 years old she has light brown skin, emerald green eyes and hair as black as the night sky. While her daughter name was Miley, she was 14 years old, had dark brown skin, golden brown eyes and beautiful brown hair. The reason they were walking in a storm with a group of people they find a cave to bunker down in a large, warm cave... but once Miley woke up the storm has past but everyone was gone all was left was a small pouch of food, water and a small amount of money with a letter that read

"To Miley we're sorry but there is to many mouths to feed in the group so we we're forced to leave you but don't worry well meet again someday but we left you some supplies to last 1day, I love you signed mother"

As Miley read tears trickled from the side of her face but, she pulled her self together and decided to look for a village after an hour she already ate the small amount of food she had got of walking until she found a small village. As she walked the stone streets but the deeper she went in the weirder feeling she got all the people weren't acting as people should they all had creepy grins and wide eyes. All while staring at the young girl she went in a store and bought a small amount of food with the little amount of money she had, as the sun set she set of to find a shelter for the night she found a small shelter to stay in for the night it was cold, wet but another for one night.

The next day the snow has melted to slush you could hear the sloshing under your boots Miley left the creepy village and went off on her way. As she walked she had the feeling something or someone was watching her, as the further she walked the weirder feeling she got "who's there" Miley said frightened but before she could do anything else she felt a large whack at the back of her head then everything went blank…

Once she woke up she was in a dark dungeon with camera's all around her she was tied firmly to a wooden chair, as she struggled she heard footsteps coming from the stairs. They were loud as thunder and far apart the scared girl was a quiet as a mouse to save herself, but it all went quiet! When she saw a large man standing before her Miley couldn't see his face because there was a long black cloak covering his full body, but what she did notice was a needle as sharp as a thorn the needle had a blue liquid inside that glowed as she struggled and screamed the needle was brought closer and closer to her arm until it was too late the needle was slowly inserted into her skin -painfully and the glowing liquid was pushed out of the syringe, as the fluid went inside her arm the tireder she got once it was all in her arm everything went black! The only thing she remembered was the man saying "you'll be home soon Miley I promise". And taking of the cloak to show his face but it was to blurry to tell what he looked like.

Once she woke up all she saw was a bright light with scientists and doctor's gathered around the young girl talking notes and talking amongst each other Miley was dressed in a white hospital gown, with a water bag attached to her arm. In a hospital she was confused and no one was answering her questions "where am I?" "Who are you?" "What's going on" once the scientists and doctors was calm as they explained Miley was in a car crash and has been I a coma for five years. Miley was to stunned to speak, so many of the people left but a doctor stayed to see if everything was fine before calling her mother. All she could think is "How was I in a coma for 5 years where was I was I in a other dimension for that long what about my mom, was the women in my mind really my mother or was it all fake."

Once her mother was called she rushed over with her father when they got there the mother ran and gave her child a hug thanking the lord for bringing her daughter. Back while her father did the same both having tears in their eyes the mother looked the same as the one in her coma! But, in the coma her father was nowhere to be seen, he still felt familiar but nether less she was happy to see her family again.

It's been 10 years since then… Miley hasn't told any one of the things she saw in her coma in fear of being seen as crazy. She still wonders who the man that brought her back was and why and wishes she could go back some time, but for now she is fine in her life now as it is.

Today's Broadcast

By Jake Evans

Welcome to BBC news this is Jake Evans today there has been a car spotted that looks like a UFO. We do not know where it's from or anything. But in China there has been spy balloons that were made to try and spy on America. But America shot some down. 2 Days later there is an update about the mysterious car. The car is believed to be made in America so that those spy balloons can't come in. There is going to be more, there's going to be more features. Like a shape shifting feature so the balloons don't get the cars. And the UFO are stronger than the cars. News update at 10pm the Chinese spy balloons have AI technology and self-assist so that the UFOs can stalk the cars were ever they are the technology is that good that they know everything. Especially facts about the person driving them and were they also live.

In America the presenter was frightened to say CNN news today at 12pm more spy balloons have come in there is fear at the moment that there is a war against America and China. President Biden has made a deal with Putin for some missiles and other weapons. Biden has made a deal with Putin which he accepted. A war has just started against America and China. China has brought balloons similar to the spy ones when they drop they cause serious damage to property and the sound is so loud that it can burst somebodies ear drums. There is a theory that it can create dark holes because it is 3x as loud as the thrust SSC. 213 people are injured and 1106 people have died to their eardrums bursting and bleeding really badly. America won the war against China. The President of China was kicked out for good and was executed. This is CNN news from 3pm.

This is Jake Evans.

Hi welcome to BBC news today there is a major update the war is ending on the 8th march 2023 and it is 16th February. And its ending in 22 days hopefully for America. 3 days pass and theres being no fighting ever since February 15th. Breaking news at 7pm China is out of spy balloons the balloons are illegal and the company has been sued 332 million yuan and the company is poor due to every single penny has been taken due to their actions.

Doors

Story By Kieron Gooding

Check page 161 for illustrator credits!

time: 10:30

date: 1968

location: first floor

<u>Prologue</u>

I was young and foolish but I should have known better than just to walk in to an abandoned hotel but here I am…..Well, I do have a name but I don't like it. I prefer to go by Jaden and this is the story of how I survived 100 doors of horror, twists, turns and MONSTERS.

Chapter 1: The first door

I just got in and all I could see was an…..elevator? Well, I guess it is normal but it looks like it's broken down. "Well I don't have much of a choice". I said as I walked in to the elevator hesitantly holding my breath hoping it would work.

To my surprise it WORKED.

"Well that was new I guess." I said as I took in my surroundings, an old registration table with suitcases and other things and…..a shadow? So there was someone else here. "HEY WAIT UP!" I shouted running up to the shadow.

The guy turned around "shhh….keep it down we don't want THEM to know we're here got it?" he whispered.

I was kind of confused but I went along with it. "Ok then…..but can you fill me in on what this place is?" I whispered.

"Well this is a hotel obviously you know that right?" He said.

"Well yea it's easy to know that."

"This isn't a normal hotel as you might have guessed" the guy said

"Ok. Is this a game of state the obvious or do you take me for an idiot?" I said annoyed.

"ugggh…..whatever one annoys you more." We stood there looking at the door…..it had a number on it….1.

"What was that supposed to mean?" I asked.

"It's door 1 what else is it meant to mean?" the guy replied.

We opened the door with a key. "I never asked what your name is?"

"Riley," he said.

"That's good to know but why are you here?" I said as we walked door to door.

We got to door 10 and then the lights started to flicker. We heard an odd sound then we both hid under beds. The lights shattered as some black mist dashed past.

"What the hell was that?" I shouted to the next room.

"How am I supposed to know?" Riley shouted back as we started to run out in to the next room and the next…..then the next…..

"How long have we been here?" I asked losing track of time.

"I don't know Sherlock you tell me." he said seeming annoyed.

I sighed "Whatever lets just….." the room went dark again but we had nowhere to hide.

"Now where can we hide?" I asked worried.

"Here's a vent. Get in," Riley shouted pulling open a vent.

We climbed in and got to the other side.

The room was dark. "good thing I have a flashlight ay?" I said.

"Sure use it" Riley said,

I turned it on and the door was at the end of a long corridor we started to walk over when one noise got my attention….

"psst," I turned around and had my eyes locked with a floating sphere

"What the-"

It let out a ear piercing screech and just vanished

"uhhh….what" I said confused on what just happened I ignored it and ran for the door and opened it the lights flicked but there was no noise. "ok then" I said confused on the fake out.

But I knew beyond that door something was lying past it just waiting for us.

Chapter 2: beyond the closed doors

Door 20 AND 21 how is that possible? "This makes no sense" I said.

"well it's a guessing game now" Riley said

We both went to door 21 we would soon know THAT WAS OUR WORST MISTAKE. We opened the door and a face was all we could see it jumped out and hit Riley hard knocking him to the floor he still got up.

Hurt yes, dead no.

"you good?" I asked

"yea I think so you?" he replied.

"well I didn't just get hit by a face so I'd say so" I said with a hint of sarcasm

We opened door 20 and walked through 6-7 doors then eyes started to appear on the walls but worst of all they were watching us as we passed through to door 30 the eyes disappeared.

"Well that was odd," I said

"You can get used to it" Riley said with confidant tone.

"wait" I said halting my movement.

"Now what?" Riley said
we both turned around to see a puddle of black slime?

"what….is that?" I asked.

"Less talking…..MORE RUNNING" Riley shouted as we started to run as the room went red.

"well ok then but why?" I shouted as we ran, ducking through chairs and book cases that fell on top of the chairs as we got further I looked behind me to see a person? No that was no man it was around 7'1 from a guess and running fast I realised IT WAS CHASING AFTER US.

"Ok NOW I know why we need to run," I shouted running faster than I thought I could.

"you didn't look back did you- HEY GET BACK HERE!" Riley shouted as

I ran past him knowing he'd most likely get killed I grabbed his arm and ran faster as chandeliers fell and hands busted out of the windows and somehow we still made it….door 50, the halfway point it was time….to really test our luck.

We heard a growl from the other side of the grand golden double doors I looked behind me "hey you ready for-" Riley wasn't there his arm must have slipped out of my hand. "you're kidding me right" I said under my breath.

"No kidding," I heard a voice behind me.

"Huh?" I turned around to see Riley?

"uhhh how?" I asked

"It's called a revive ever heard of one" he replied

"Who does the what now?" I said in a fit of confusion.

"God you really are dumb aren't ya?" he said annoyed.

"Whatever you say Mr I'm so perfect," I said with a cocky tone to my voice we both looked at the doors.

"ready?" I asked

"Sure I am," Riley replied as we pushed the double doors open to reveal a library we then heard the growl again as a loud stomp and a fleshy looking foot we knew we were in for a challenge.

This time there was no turning back now.

The Clown who Drowned

Story By Layton Carney
Check page 161 for illustrator credits!

There was a boy called Bill, who was on a school trip to a deep, dark, deadly forest. He heard a loud shout far away. He was confused, so he decided to search until he found the most beautiful lake in the entire world. He shouted for his class to see this beautiful lake, but no response. He saw a skeleton in the water wearing a clown costume, Bill was shocked, the clown was Bill's grandfather. Bill looked at the clown's back there were scars writing in scrambled numbers: 20 8 5 12 9 5 19 12 9 22 5 9 14 13 5. Bill was confused then suddenly… the hand of the corpse grabbed Bill's leg, the clown rises from the lake Bill screamed as loud as he could.

The class were searching for him then they came across the lake, but Bill wasn't there! The class saw bubbles coming from the surface. One of the student's jumped in the lake the student was shocked, there was an old circus under the lake, the student found a piece of Bill's shirt, the student swam to the surface to tell the class a terrifying scene he saw…

The Voice

By Lucas Bryan

I'm Aiden, a 17 year old boy who still doesn't know who he wants to be. I still live with in my parents' house and I have a problem. I hear a voice in my head and it always blocks out my thoughts and everything else around me. It says weird things like "You are not normal!" and "You are meant to blend in with them, not become one of them!"

I worry about what it all means. The voice has been with me all of my life. It was the first voice that I heard and will probably be the last. Back then the voice was just a normal voice of a girl that I had never met before but recently, the voice has been getting more and angrier.

Today her voice has been excited, even happy. I woke up feeling my muscles aching as I walk out of my room. I look out of the window and I saw something flying in the sky. A type of space craft maybe? It was black with subtle hints of purple then I thought… If this is a dream, thank God. If this is real then I am probably going to die soon!

The voice screamed with a shriek of excitement. "It's time!"

A mechanical arm shot out and wrapped its pincers around me and then retracted, pulling me in while breaking through the window. I started to move faster than a moving train at max speed. And just like that, I was in. The arm let go of me and I was being carried by humanoid life forms with longer arms and legs and they were covered in black liquid, like a combination of ink and slime.

Oddly enough, I could understand what they were saying and translate the words.

"Bring him to the infusion."

"What?" "Don't they recognise me?"

The voice lashed out "No, no no I am not losing this body!"

I started to feel sick, then pain then nothing at all as my vision fades into darkness. The voice spoke once more.

"Hey. Stop right now!"

"Why should we?"

"I'm Linda 0746 now let me down!"

My vision was starting to return.

"Ah, Linda wasn't expecting you to last this long. Now hand over the info. Drive."

I asked myself "what?" I accidentally said it out loud. I started to hit my head uncontrollably saying "shut up human!!!"

She was controlling me. But how? And why has this never happened before after all of these years? My hand turned black and phased out through my head. My vision went grey and blurry. I felt dead…but I was still alive, right?

The hand retracted, holding a type of chip. I seem to be some kind of robot.

A black sludge pulled itself out of my body. The voice was gone.

Linda was a leech and I was her host. I am now just a lifeless host.

I want to live…Please!

Boom.

The floor beneath us shattered and before long an alarm started to ring throughout the ship. The guards ran to their work stations but Linda just stood there with the chip in her hand.

"Please, just one more year Linda!"

She looked at me with a stare that looked through my soul…well, what's left of it.

"Fine, but after that you are dead meat!"

"I already am."

Her hand fazed through my head and re-installed the chip. My eyesight was restored and I felt alive again.

"Hand!"

The arm wrapped around me again and I was thrust back out. It violently dropped me on the pavement and recoiled.

Military jets started to fly around the ship, shooting rapidly.

The ship turned to the sky and fired into space.

A fighter jet landed near me and a man walked out and approached me.

"Are you OK sir?"

"I think so." I replied.

A Colourful Walk

By Lucille

Dedicated to Mr Mac

With thanks to Amelia, Rosie, Esme, Mummy, Daddy, Albert & Edwin.

"Ella, we're doing it for your own good!" She was annoyed with her parents. She always had to wear black and white. It didn't make sense, how could it be for her own good? Ella (who was 10) was not an only child. She had two younger sisters, Chloe (8) and Tilly (1). They had pale faces with dark hair and unusual monobrows.

The sisters were very good friends. Their mum and dad didn't pick them up or drop them off at school, they walked home together every day before they went swimming. They were very good swimmers. They swam 5 lengths (125m) every day. They also all liked being outside and colourful things like bright sunflowers and scarlet-red poppies. Their parents only liked black and white with an occasional dash of orange.

When they got home, Chloe brought out a game to play with Tilly in the garden while eating ice pops. Tilly was crawling around and licking her ice pop. They were trying to join in with Tilly but the game was a bit boring. There was a meadow near the house that had lots of bright wild flowers. They always wanted to go there but their parents always said no. They didn't like colour. Chloe said they could sneak away and Ella agreed. They headed off and found themselves in the meadow.

When they got to the meadow, they were surprised by all the different flowers in the meadow. They passed a brilliant, fluttering, butterfly. They also passed a chirping, shy bird. They saw a nimble squirrel shimmying up the hollow tree. They soon saw a red carpet of bright, wild poppies. There were a few Welsh poppies as well. They collected some of the soft, delicate petals. Among the leaves, some grass-green clovers were hiding within the flowers. They got some of the clovers. Next they saw some fine papery forget-me-nots and put them into their basket. Soon they saw in the distance that there were some elegant flowers. As they got closer they discovered that next to the thistles were some intense, vibrant yellow buttercups. Soon they passed some deep blue cornflowers. They collected a few of each flower and put it in the basket.

"That's enough" declared Chloe.

"One more!" pleaded Ella.

"Oh, Ok!" "No need to shout!" said Chloe.

"Sure, we can have one more," responded Chloe.

"Chloe, what do you think we should do with all this?" Asked Ella.

"I'm not sure, we could make some things like; necklaces, bracelets, headbands?" replied Chloe.

"Good point, my only issue with that is what about mum and dad?" questioned Ella.

"Let's go home, we'll risk it, what's the worst that could happen? "said Chloe.

"They could stop us from having fish fingers" retaliated Ella.

"We should go back home now" "It's getting dark" continued Chloe.

"Yes, I agree, mum and dad might get worried!" agreed Ella

***

When they got home, they hole punched the petals for necklaces and bracelets. They put pins in clovers and buttercups so they could make earrings and broaches. They got a plain headband and weaved the blue flowers (the buttercups and cornflowers) in and out. They threaded a thistle onto a hair clip. They hid them all in a box so their parents could not see all the vibrant colours.

The next day they woke up to a bright and sunny morning. It was Monday.

"How are we going to go to school with out getting into trouble with the flowers in the box?" wondered Chloe next morning.

"I know!" exclaimed Ella with excitement.

"What's your plan?" asked Chloe.

"My plan is to leave it in our TOP SECRET FOLDER" responded Ella.

"Great idea," stated Chloe.

"I thought so too," remarked Ella.

At school it felt like ages until breaktime when they were going to talk about how they were going to show mum and dad their love of colour. At last, it was breaktime. They agreed to go up to their bedroom and put on all of their vivid coloured accessories. What could possibly go wrong? After all, they're just accessories!

***

When they got home they went upstairs and took out the top secret folder. They opened it up and saw all of the eye catching flowers. They stared at them for a while and then, being very careful they lifted up all of the accessories one by one. They helped one another to get them on very carefully.

"It's tea time" called Mum in a shrill voice.

"Coming in a minute!" Ella shouted.

Quickly, they put on some of the accessories on each other and went downstairs, trembling with worry and a little bit of excitement.

"Girls, what are you wearing?" yelled Mum and Dad in a unison.

"It's just a bit of colour isn't it?" questioned Chloe.

"Does it look like a little bit?" asked Dad.

"Is it necessary?" added Mum.

"Yes" said Ella with a hint of anger in her voice.

"Why would it be necessary?" asked Mum.

"Does it have to be necessary?" responded Ella.

"Exactly!" replied Chloe.

Mum and Dad exchanged glances.

"Ok, I suppose we don't have to be so dull", said Dad.

"Although I do like the bright orange flowers!" said Mum.

"Hooray"" cheered both girls loudly at the same time.

"You know we are still Humboldt but if you feel colourful that's fine" declared Dad.

Note: Humboldt Penguins are medium sized penguins. They are coloured black or dark grey on their back and white on their front. They have a distinctive, black, horseshoe shaped band on their front and a white stripe on their head. They live in South America unlike other penguins who live in cold conditions and in the water they can swim at speeds of up to 20 miles per hour. They have no orange but some other species of penguins do such as Emperor Penguins and Rockhoppers.

Rebecca's Gaming Adventure

By Rebecca Snaith

Hi, My name is Rebecca!

I was once playing on my computer when there was a big flash. I thought it was nothing, I thought it was part of my game when all of a sudden a *BIG BOOM*!!

I was sucked into my computer it was like in a time travel, all loopy and swirly and dizzy, I thought I was being drunk!

But no I was actually here in my computer in my videogame. I was so scared I landed in mud all yucky and sticky. Sworms climbed up my leg, I shook my leg so the sworms come off my leg! I looked around, and there was sand everywhere, mud puddles and huge mythical plants with large pink flowers that open and shoot out poison that kill when it touches skin. I started to run, I heard voices, I stopped and there it was! Wolf talking to me!

I was in shock, I started to talk back my voice shaking.

She said her name was Athena, she's here to help me as I MUST defeat the dragacorn. Athena takes me to her pack I could still hear the voices in my head. I said "I am going insane."

Athena said "no, we can communicate with you inside your mind, it's a good thing don't worry! We're here now, this is my home!" said Athena.

"That's my pack, you see him over there? That's the Alpha. We call him the Shadow-hunter. He hunts in the night with his shadow friends."

Athena took me over to the alpha. He said "Who are you and what are you doing here?!" he said.

I said "I was sucked into my game."

"I see," he said.

"Can you help me please? I need to defeat the Dragacorn. Please I need your help so I can go back to the real world!"

"I will help if you help us?"

"Okay whatever you need."

"You need to go far away to get some food for us. We can't leave our home it's in danger so we need to stay here. I will let Athena come with you to show you the way but after that you're all alone. We will communicate with you in your mind but be careful out there! It's dangerous."

"Thanks! Come on, we'd better get going then. So how did I get into this world then?"

Athena said "it was a curse, it sometimes happens to everyone but they don't make it out alive."

"So where were yous?" then I said.

"We weren't here," said Athena.

"May I ask, were you human once?"

"YES!"

"I'm so sorry," I said.

"It's okay… Here we are, you're on your own now, be safe to you!"

I was walking all by myself, I keep hearing noises in the trees and bushes and all of a sudden something BIG came out!!

"BOOOOOO!"

I screamed "AAAAAAAA!"

"Hello," the strange creature said.

"Hi," I said. "What are you meant to be?"

"I am a monkey mixed with a barn owl. My name is Betty!"

"Nice to meet you!"

"Nice to meet you too!"

"What's your name?"

"My name is Rebecca! I have reached the top of the mountains, I've got it!" I said.

"Good, come quick, the Dragacorn is here! okay, I'm on my way!"

I rushed to the village. "Athena are you okay?"

"Yeah am fine. Quick drink this!"

"What is it?"

"It will make you strong!"

I drink it.

"How do you feel?"

"I feel normal." And all of a sudden I grew strong! I was fighting the Dragacorn, he scratched my face, blood pouring out, and *BOOOOM* off with your head Dragacorn!

Everyone was cheering on, I saved everyone!

"Thank you! I have to go now, I will visit again don't worry!"

And everyone was safe and sound.

The Scream of Terror

By Nathan Berry

Deep down under-ground there was once an abandoned laboratory, during 1970 it had workers at every possible angle making a fun little TV show, a reality show that was loved by kids all over the world "rebel and friends" a funny TV show that had a cast of colorful characters such as Rebel the rabbit, Sam the snake and Camo the cat and way more. But, after an experiment gone wrong the only thing remaining is a never ending laboratory filled with a variety of creatures.

42 years after the facility was abandoned, left to rot one cryptozoologist was interested and decided to take a visit. Once the cryptozoologist also known as Daniel got to the place, they took out an old rusty camera and filmed every second he was there. He encountered some strange things a pipe sticking out the wall with claw marks another being a giant teddy bear.

Why would that be in a place like this? he wondered after 2 or 3 hours starting to lose hope he heard some strange clanking noises that sounded like something was trying to open an elevator with hands. Daniel followed the noise thinking he was onto something, he went around a corner and saw a very tall green cat that looked similar to one of the characters from the show... it was Camo the cat. Camo turned around and made eye contact with Daniel, as soon as Daniel was about to start filming again Camo opened his mouth revealing a row of very sharp triangle shaped teeth and charged towards Daniel like a cat running towards a mouse ready to consume it.

Daniel was running the fastest he ever did in his life! Knowing if Camo catches him it'll be his end. Daniel turned around while running and saw Camo on all fours totally faster than Daniel, after 6 minutes he found a distraction. Daniel caused a fire behind him stopping Camo from getting through well that's what he thought anyway… he looked back and he saw a glimpse of Camo ripping a vent door off its hinges and jumps in. After a few more minutes trembling about the fact if Camo knew where he was Daniel finds a note sitting in a workspace from someone named Terry. He couldn't tell what the note was saying since most of it was scribbled but judging off what he could find it seems Terry was planning something. But it wasn't known what it was since scribbles were blocking most of the note Daniel took a photo on his camera of the note then he continued on his journey. Daniel was confused, since the place was honestly just a never ending maze after an hour or more he took a left turn to another hallway but he felt this hard punch over the head Daniels vision slowly became darker and darker!

Daniel woke up after his hard punch, he was in a room tied to a chair with candles surrounding the chair, and the door was blocked so he couldn't leave. He looked to the other side of the room in the shadows he saw a humanoid figure with its hands behind its back the figure came from the shadows his appearance was weird it was a gray boiler suit with a mask covering his face the mask was a purple rabbit with pitch black eyes, with red pupils his arm came out from behind his back to see an axe. The armed man started to talk "well what is this here another outsider."

Daniel asked "who are you?"

The man responded with "I am Terry." Daniel eventually noticed "And you are the next sacrifice," Terry said, adding onto what he was saying.

Moments after Terry said that he heard something coming from behind him Daniel turned behind him to see a vent getting flung off the wall to slide across the floor, a giant robotic claw scraped across the wall leaving claw marks, another hand comes out from the vent then a head a weird shaped robot head with no eyes but the thing that was off about it is that it didn't look like any of the characters from the show. Daniel got shivers down his spine the robot monster leaped onto Daniel the next thing that happened was a huge scream of terror!

Camping

By Riley Dunn

Chapter 1:

Day 0

Mr Turner says to the class "Alright class we're going to a camping trip today… I hope you brought your belongings with you." Then Mr Turner started to count and name the students. "Okay we've got Jake, Kyle, Kieran, Joseph and Müller. Also William, Dominic, Daniel, David and Lucas." He said curiously as he check them.

"Is everyone ready?" he replied loudly.

The class replied "We're ready sir." The teacher smiled then the bus door opened.

"Everyone inside!"

They got inside the bus and placed their suitcases above their heads and sat down where they felt comfortable.

The teacher looked outside too see that no one was left outside but little does he know, he left William behind when he went to the toilet without telling him. Then just from the distance "Wait for me!" Shouted William.

The teacher chuckled to himself and said "We almost left you there c'mon and get inside the bus." William hurried inside of the bus.

"Sorry everyone for your time." He apologised to everyone on the bus then placed his suitcase above him and sat down on his seat.

Chapter 2:

Where it all began

After long hours on the bus we eventually made it to the camp site. "Alright Class get your suitcases." Mr Turner said to the class. Everyone started to grab their suitcases then head over to the camp site.

Mr Turner grabbed out two big camping tents that were coloured yellow and green "Alright class help me out with building the tents." Said Mr Turner kindly.

Everyone started to help Mr Turner set up the big tents and they eventually finished in 18 minutes then everyone started to grab their suitcases then unpacked them inside the tents.

Mr Turner grabbed the sleeping bag from his bag "Does anyone want some marshmallows?" He asked them.

"I do!" shouted William.

"Of course you want some." Mr Turner chuckled to himself.

***

As the day slowly turned to night, everyone was sitting around the campfire with sticks and marshmallows. They told themselves creepy made up stories around the Flaming hot fire.

"One stormy night a family of 5 went on a camping trip in these woods they we're just minding their business setting up their tent… Later that night dark in the woods something was outside walking and breathing. The family went outside the tent it was the biggest mistake of their lives." As the teacher stopped everyone stood still and was shaking.

"Is everyone alright? Did I scare you all?" He said curiously.

"Look behind you!" William shouted.

The teacher laughed

"Stop joking around William." He said to William.

"No look behind you!" He said again.

The teacher turned around and his face was left blank then saw something that he shouldn't have seen in his lifetime.

Everyone screamed then started to run in 1 direction.

Mr Turner froze as he couldn't move then a weird creature grabbed him by the legs then dragged him into the darkness of the forest never too be see again "Wait I think their might be a cave nearby." Said William to the class

"Where?!" shouted Kieran.

"Just follow me." Said William calmly.

William pulled out the map for the camping site he made it eventually reached to the cave.

"We made it!" Shouted Dominic.

"Shhhh!" Said everyone.

The class went inside the cave as it had started to rain outside.

"Well that was weird." Said Müller with a Swiss accent

Someone's stomach growled loudly.

"Where's the basket?" Said Kyle.

Everyone groaned that they left the basket of sandwiches outside the cave

"I'll get them!" Said Kyle heroically.

He went outside the cave and started to head back to the camp then spotted a basket of sandwiches.

"I found it!" Said Kyle then he headed back to the cave all soaking wet

"I'm back!" Said Kyle.

Everyone smiled then Kyle opened the basket of sandwiches then every chose one that they selected then started to eat them.

"Wait." Said joseph.

"Why?" Said everyone.

"The sandwich tastes like they have been poisoned." Said Joseph.

Joseph suddenly was foaming from the mouth then slammed down onto the ground.

"Joseph!" Shouted William.

Everyone ran over to him to see if he was ok but he had stopped breathing.

"He's gone" Said William.

Then all of a sudden the ground was shaking

"Earthquake!" Said Müller with his Swiss accent.

The rocks came falling down from the roof and blocked off the cave entrance.

"It's dark." Said Lucas.

William got out his phone then turned torch mode on.

He spotted Daniel in front of him and shone the light on him.

"You scared me!" Said William.

Daniel shrugged his shoulders then turned to the wall.

"Hey! There's light coming from the crack of the wall." Said Daniel.

William went over, knocked on the wall and it crumbled into pieces.

"Whoa!" Said William

Chapter 3:

Day 1

The crumbled wall revealed a secret corridor. The class approached it cautiously.

"Follow me." Said William

Everyone followed him then saw 2 slides .David approached the slide on the right side.

"Wish me luck." Said David.

He went down the slide then the class heard a thump.

"David!" yelled William.

David didn't respond so the class went through the left tunnel

Everyone slid down the slide one at a time then blood dripped from the ceiling of the roof.

"Is that… blood?"

He noticed that it could have been David's but the class continued walking then a black figure appeared from the corner.

"You…" Said William.

The creature walked through the corridor then went around the corner

William started to chase after the creature then he turned the corner.

"Where is that creature?" He yelled loudly.

Daniel fell to the ground then started to slowly breathe.

"Daniel?" Said Jake.

As soon as Jake went over to Daniel the roof collapsed blocking off the corridor.

Everyone ran to the top then saw light from outside then water started flowing.

"Head back to the campsite!"

Everyone started to run back to the campsite but the water was dragging them.

"Climb up here!" Said William.

William grabbed Lucas then made him fall onto the ground causing him to bang his head onto a rock that killed him.

Chapter 4:

Betrayal

As everyone reached the top of the pillar William grabbed Dominic then pulled him off the ladders.

"Have a nice swim." Said William.

"You're a murderer." Said The Monster.

Space-time Prehistory

By Rowan

A boy was walking through some dense, dark and deadly woods, as a rockslide fell from the cliff above him! Almost crushing the boy. The boy's name was Bill he just barely escaped and climbed up the cliff. This allowed him the see the rift to a space-time pocket dimension… with dinosaurs and other prehistoric creatures from different periods of time, living in a sustained ecosystem. Plus they can speak English or he could just understand them! Out of the cave next to him a Tyrannosaurus Rex tried to eat him (since they knew about humans) but a Tropeognathus who called himself Dave saved him and flew him up past the clouds where he was safe.

"You're welcome kid by the way, yes I only eat fish who are you?" said Dave.

"I'm Bill," The boy replied "So can you help me survive till I can go through the portal again Dave?"

"Sure I'd love to help you out Bill," said Dave.

As they landed a group as Heterodontosaurus were being chased by a Carnotaurus which in turn was being chased by a Carcharadontosaurus, who then ran seeing the magnificent shining purple and gold scales of the Tropeognathus in front of him as the other creatures passed him as a Liopruodon and Elasmosaurus swam through the water.

Then the same T-rex came crashing through the trees as the Carnotaurus helped Dave kill the Tyrannosaur as he said it was called Derek a dinosaur who just killed for sport not to live.

As a sort of spear of energy crashed into the ground after two months of making weapons and surviving, Bill who was about to leave when he saw the portal was stopped by Dave who as Bill wasn't looking at him said he wanted to say something. But as Bill turned to Dave, he was killed and discarded to the human world and it was thought he was attacked by a wolf and was buried but Dave did this so that his world was never discovered but another spear of energy hit Dave killing him! But sealing that world away forever and carnage broke out allowing tiny bits of energy to escape into space in our dimension as a black hole opened in the middle of the universe from this happening...

Then after that some sort of 4th dimensional being started to emerge from this black hole seeming to be seeking something...

The End

A Surprising Adventure

By Brandon Low, Demi Hill and Ryan Bell

Once upon a time three friends went to visit their local toyshop. They had been hundreds of times before but this time it was completely different!

John picked up a Thomas train and immediately it came to life; whistling, huffing and puffing.

Suddenly, John shrank to the size of one of the toy soldiers on the shelf nearby. Cameron and Rose were surprised and a bit frightened. "What's going on?" shouted Cameron.

Just then Rose picked up a picnic basket; as she did, the food became real – crunchy, red apples, melted cheese and delicious bars of chocolate.

In a flash Rose shrank too.

By this time Cameron was spooked. "I wonder what will happen if I pick up this book?" thought Cameron.

As soon as he touched it, the book flipped open to the picture of a map. He too shrank to the same size as John and Rose.

"Let's go!" shouted John. "I've worked out how to drive this thing!"

"Where are we going?" asked Rose.

Cameron said, "I've got a map of London. Let's go there."

Cameron and Rose loaded the coal while John sat himself in the cab. "Here we go!" he yelled.

Soon Cameron and Rose's faces were hot and sweaty and covered in soot. "This is hard work, I'm tired!" moaned Rose.

"Soon be there," said John. "I can see the palace."

"Let's go to the London Eye," said Rose excitedly. "You can see right across the city. It's a brilliant view."

"It's this way," said Cameron pointing to his left.

Suddenly, Rose let out a squeak as someone's foot almost squashed her. "It's really scary being this small. We need to be careful."

Out of the corner of his eye, John spotted a dog. "We could jump on the dog to keep us safe."

They all jumped onto the dog's tail and climbed onto its back.

"Grab onto its collar and hold tight," shouted Rose.

"What's happening? Who are you?" growled the dog.

John got such a shock that he let go of the dog's collar and almost slid off.

Cameron grabbed his arm and helped him back up.

"You can talk?" said John in surprise.

"Obviously! Don't all dogs?"

"Not where we come from," answered John.

"Can you help us?" asked Rose. "We want to get to the London Eye but we're too little and worried in case we get squashed."

"Not a problem." Replied the dog whose name was Clifford.

After five minutes, they all arrived at the London Eye.

"Oh no, we haven't got any money; we won't be able to buy a ticket." Said Cameron sadly.

"Let's try and sneak on." Suggested Rose.

"I won't be able to join you, said Clifford. "It's been lovely to meet you. I hope you get home safely."

"Thank you so much for the ride. It was really fun." Said John.

Just then, a man with turn-up trousers stood next to them in the queue.

Rose nudged the others. "Look! We could climb into those turn-ups. Nobody would notice."

Carefully, they each climbed in.

The view from the wheel was amazing. The sun was shining brightly and they could see for miles.

Suddenly, John spotted Thomas waiting for them below, When they got off at the bottom, Thomas said crossly, "Well grind my axles. Where have you been? I've been looking everywhere for you!"

Suddenly, there was panic.

"Fire! Fire!" They heard someone yell. "Press the fire bell."

"Quick, we need to get out of here," shouted Cameron.

"Run!" yelled Rose.

***

"…Wake up Rose, wake up" said a voice.

Rose rubbed her eyes and peered up at the face leaning over her. "You were shouting. We're you having a bad dream?"

"Mum?"

"We're you having a bad dream? You're alarm has just gone off. It's time to get ready for school.

Sophie's Strategy

By Ashton Bell

Monday 7th September was an ordinary start to the school day apart from one thing, A new student joined our class. She was called Sophie and liked Art. Initially, she was quite quiet but once she began to make friends, soon came out of her shell.

One thing did stand out; she was not a genius and was a pretty average student. Being in a class of geniuses was a bit hard and she soon fell behind the rest of her peers.

This became more obvious as the school year progressed. Sophie became really sad as no matter how hard she studied, she could never catch them up. Until one day everything changed…

Our class had completed a series of mock exams and we were awaiting our results. As Sophie got her papers back, we were all expecting her to look depressed and disappointed as she read her marks. Slowly she turned the paper over and her face lit up. She had aced the exam! The rest of us had done well but hadn't received 100%. What was going on? She had gone from being an average student to excelling in every subject. She couldn't have copied because we had all got lower scores. She couldn't have memorised every single piece of information as we didn't know what the questions were going to be. Something was going on, but what? Had Mrs Stephenson helped her? No, that can't be right, she would never do something like that?

The next day in lessons, no sooner had Mrs Stephenson written the question on the board, Sophie had answered them instantly and correctly. We were all shocked to see that they were right and she couldn't have even had time to think.

This continued over the next few weeks until we had a cover teacher. Sophie looked horrified. Did she know her? Was she an old teacher from her past that she disliked? Was that the deal?

We settled down to work. Sophie barely scraped through the work. She was back to how she was when she first joined our class. Everyone was confused. What was going on?

This happened a few times over the term. Most days, Sophie displayed top level skills. She could have taught the class herself! But on the odd occasion she reverted to barely being able to complete the work.

Over time a pattern began to form. The days the cover teacher was in were the days Sophie completed average work; but the days Mrs Stephenson was in she completed work in record time often allowing time for her to practise her chess skills while the rest of us finished.

One day she was playing Mrs. Stephenson. Sophie seemed to to always be one step ahead. "It's almost as if you can read my mind," commented our teacher.

Sophie's whole body tensed and her face turned bright red.

Suddenly, I realised the truth. Mrs Stephenson had hit the nail on the head. Why hadn't I realised before? Instead of teacher's reading students' minds, this student could read our teacher's mind!

"The games up, Sophie," said Mrs Stephenson. I think that's checkmate!

The Magical Dream of Sweets

By Neave Smith, Heidi Stott, Lewis Newman and Lilia Searle

Once upon a time, there was a girl called Alice who owned a shop at The Metrocentre. This shop had beautiful pastel colours which was very inviting because of the wonderful smells which were coming from the freshly made sweets.

Suddenly, the Queen of Hearts appeared from nowhere. She sneaked down the biscuit aisle and quickly grabbed the lemon sherbets from the shelf.

Alice saw the Queen of Hearts stealing the sweets. She began shouting, "Shop stealer! Shop stealer!" to the security guard.

The security guard came running and arrested the Queen of Hearts.

All of a sudden, The Queen of Hearts took a small cake from her pocket. Taking a huge bite, she vanished into thin air.

The security guard looked around shocked and surprised that she had suddenly disappeared…

Waking with a start, Alice woke up and realised it had been one bad dream.

The Return

By Thomas L

After a five year long holiday at the countryside I was finally returning to London. It had been such a long time I almost forgot what my house looked like, I couldn't wait to see my mum and dad as I haven't got a letter from them since last Christmas.

I just couldn't hold my excitement to the point where I wished the train would speed up or drop one of the carriages at the back so there's less weight dragging the train down. After a couple of hours the sun had set and the moon raised, most of the other passengers were asleep but I was still awake my excitement going to sleep was something my body refused to do.

So I stared out the window for a while at the valley of grass lit up by the blinding moon light, I could see a group of owls flying around the obstacle course of trees that was the forest it reminded me of the air planes that would zoom past the village from time to time.

Finally after one whole day and night we arrived at the London train station, when the train doors opened I raced out the doors hoping to see my mum and dad but they weren't there so I waited and waited to where I was the only person waiting in the train station.

After twenty minutes of waiting I saw my uncle running over to me the first thing I asked him was where mum and dad were. He said the war wasn't kind to many people, many of them got hurt really badly. Your mum and dad got hurt really bad so they have joined god in heaven to get better.

I asked him if I would ever see them again he didn't answer my question and just hugged me and started crying.

The Girl in the Sewer

By Tillie Emma McDonald

Once there was a rich, kind and inquisitive girl. She was on a walk with her family…

When men with masks jumped out of a bush they pointed guns at us and said "give us all your money!" my parents did what they asked but they… still shot them. I was stood in shock they shoved me in a pile of wet mud.

I went back to my house and the guards would not let me in they said you don't look like a family member of this household they kicked me out. My dad said something before he got shot, he said "I worked with bad people they after me for my money, you need to run when you see anyone wearing masks and black clothes, Or they will take you to their boss there boss is an evil man! Don't let them catch you!"

So I ran as fast as I could but then I fell in to a hole… it was a sewer, I landed in water dirty water, I walked and walked and then I heard my name being called the bad guys I thought they did not know my name. But, I was wrong they know my name, at the time I thought it was my guards so I ran and ran. When I got to them then I saw it was the boss and the bad guys. The bad guys grabbed me and I screamed then, this boy came out of nowhere and swung from the vines hanging off the pipes above us like a monkey.

He grabbed my hand and I lifted up in the air and got away, it felt like I was flying. The boy introduced his self his name was Andy. Andy lives in the sewer he's an orphan he ran away so he's being living in the sewers for two years. We are both 14 years old.

He asked me "why are those guys after you?" he asked. Andy said "they are not bad people they are look after my daughter!"

"No!" I said. "you must be wrong!"

He replied "I am not maybe you should go and see them they are looking for you!"

"Ok," I said, he came with me we reached the bad guys and the boss give me a hug.

I was confused I said "what are you doing?"

He replied "I am you dad!"

I freaked out "NO YOUR'RE NOT! My dad got shot by your people and my mother did too!"

he replied "No they took you when you were a baby we have being looking and looking for you."

I was so confused I asked "where is my mum?" then he told me… "she is in the hospital she in a coma", he showed me photos and I believed him. He took me to my new house my mother finally woke up and my father and mother adopted Andy!

The end

The Robotics Company

By Anonymous

William Afton Robotics- he makes robots to entertain children but he has a family of two or three. The crying child, his brothers took him to a room with animatronic suits. He looks around the room for a flashlight and he found one but its battery is half full so he found a mask and so he can hear.

The twist is he's wearing a suit that's been worn for 25 years and it smells like rotten flesh. He can't breathe or even walk.

The Sailor

By Kai C

Once upon a time there was a sailor called Popeye who was strong. And do you know how he was strong? He was Strong! He ate lots of spinach and that's why he's so strong but after a couple of days he was fuzzy. Feeling his eyes open.

But… It was a dream!

He wasn't strong anymore.

Lexi and Puggy

By Lexi Hall

Once upon a time there was a teenage girl called Lexi and she had a teddy called Puggy. Lexi loved Puggy very much and she used to take him everywhere but now he stays in Lexi's room every day.

Puggy didn't mind at all because every day when Lexi goes outside Puggy comes to life and all the other teddies do and sometimes they have a party and have lots of fun!

The teddies could also talk to each other and sometimes they sneak out and go places to have lots of fun.

But that's not all! What if they had a teddy school and Puggy was the teacher and they were planning to go places they had never been before! And maybe Puggy can drive so they can go travel with a car and maybe Lexi's mam and dad look after Puggy when Lexi is at school.

The End by Lexi and Puggy

Scary Story

By Michael Hackett

This is a story I still can't get over. As I type this I'm scared if he will come back. I'm on high alert. When I was 10 my next door neighbour John was arrested.

He creeped me out. He stared at me as I came home. I wouldn't call him what you're thinking but he acted like one at times.

I wanted to punch him. He was so ugly and weird. I don't know why but he always rambled on and on about me. I was creeped. The night they arrested him I felt relieved.

My mum was crying. I asked why,, she simply did not speak and closed the door. I thought, *what just happened?*

Next day I got up. My mum was sitting at the table and her face was happy but also sad. I asked my mum again to which she again blanked it, excusing herself from the table.

To the present I now know what happened which I never knew before. So I googled the house and the neighbours. Turns out John had died not 4 years ago, about 40 years ago. He was 64 and his body was removed at 32 years of decomposition so I'd not witnessed a man getting arrested. I'd witnessed a man getting removed dead.

It ain't over, he's staring right now as I type this.

I'm 14 and he is at the window staring at me and that's impossible. He's dead. I'm scared.

My mum came through the door and screamed. She took me out of the bedroom I sleep in.

What happened next I can only describe as horrible. We screamed as we left to escape the house. And there's John, just being creepy as he always was. Only difference was his smile came on and I did not like it.

It screamed trouble but all of a sudden it disappeared. In front of me are eyes.

I was completely confused, so not only is this a creepy man, but also a dead man and a ghost. Not what you would expect and not what I would expect.

But he's gone for now.

10:40pm

I'm trying to tell you all is fine but—

Casino

By Scotty Berry

In the morning a bell started ringing. Harry, Zac, Dave and Kate boarded home from school. They stopped and saw a medium sized poster.

They looked at it and saw a casino.

Zac says "wow lets go to casino!"

The Dave: "okay!"

Story By Lucas Ransom

Check page 161 for illustrator credits!

I've heard of this place called 'The sea'. My great uncle Michael used to tell me stories of his adventures in it when I was just 1 month old. He is 2 and ¾ now and he said that 'The Sea' is a great place full of all different kinds of creatures. Most importantly though there is no plastic in it. Not one piece. The river we live in has almost no clear area and I can only imagine how wonderful it must be to have clear water surrounding you. I have had enough of the mucky, dirty rubbish filled place I call home.

I told my parents, "I'm leaving and there's nothing you can say that will change my mind."

And so I went. I swam away downstream, away from my family, away from my life. It wasn't easy having to push past all the rubbish. I must have been swimming when I encountered the first obstacle: a dam built by a beaver. It looked old and disused with pieces of twig and log loosely floating in the water around it.

I tried to squeeze myself through on of the many tiny holes. I won't give up I mustn't give up I thought. Finally 'pop' I went flying through the hole into the water beyond. I was about to set off again when something caught the corner of my eye. A beaver!

I tried to swim away but it was too late. I felt his warm hands catch onto my long tail. As hard as I swam I could not get out of the beaver's vice like grip. Eventually after a lot of flailing I was pulled from the water into the air.

Black spots began to appear in the corners of my eyes as I began to lose consciousness. I had one last chance to break free before I suffocated or I was eaten. I flailed my tail one last time and, unbelievably, I slipped from its grip and fell right back into the polluted water with a loud SPLASH. Without a second thought I swam as fast as my orange tail would take me.

'I'm not food today!'

Then I saw some food just sitting there waiting to be eaten. I forgot all about how I had been told to never not eat random food because more times than not it was a human trying to eat you. I bit into the delicious food and felt something cold and hard hit the top of my mouth. It was suddenly jerked upwards and I felt a terrible pain on my lip as it caught me.

I should have listened to the advice. As I went higher and higher out of the water I thought I would never stop going up even though it was just seconds it felt like hours to me.

Eventually I stopped flying and came back down to earth and was whisked up into a bright red bucket. I thought I would never escape and I should just give up hope. When it started to get dark I was finally released.

Free at last, I started up again on my journey. Not long after the river widened so far I could not see the edge. My great uncle Michael had said that when the river is this wide it must be 'the sea'. At first I was confused.

'This can't be the sea, it is not clean!' As far as the eye could see it was littered with junk. Deep down I knew that it was the sea.

After 2 years the sea had gotten just as bad as the river.

The Queen and the Jungle Thief

By Felicity McMurtary

Chapter One: The Call

I had just finished calling my mate Brian and was heading up to his house when I noticed that his cat was trying to scare me off! It was just so weird.

But then I noticed that she had a scratch on her nose and wasn't trying to scare me off. She was trying to ask for help. She was struggling with the pain. I need to help her and fast! So I knocked on the door and Brian came to the door to greet me.

"Ummmmm…" I said, "Do you know that your cat is injured? She needs to get to the vets and fast! She has a large, bleeding scratch on her nose."

"I didn't know, I will get her to the vets as soon as possible." Brian said, in a panic. "Thank you" and he drove off with me in the back.

After the vets, I was speaking to Brian and I said "you know I came here this very night to tell you I got a call from the Queen saying to meet us in the Jungle! She has a top secret mission for us!"

"WOW!" Said Brian. "Let's go tomorrow."

"Or next week?" I suggested, feeling scared. "It's a big thing, we need to prepare. You know what I mean?"

"Silly me. I got a bit over excited there." Replied Brian.

Chapter Two: The Big Pack

It was morning and I was getting ready to pack for the big adventure to go to the jungle to meet the Queen! We leave tomorrow. I walked into the dining room and set out some bags on the table and set to work. First, I went to the living room and got some really comfy cushions and a bean bag. And then I walked to the dining room and put them in the bag. Next, I walked to the kitchen and collected some flannels and an apron. I also picked up some food, including a slice of cake and a salad to keep me going for the journey. Then, I went to the bathroom to collect some toilet rolls and to the study to pick up a few books and some paper to draw on. Next, I went to the medicine cupboard and packed a medical bag. In it I had, amongst other things, love and emergency chocolate.

After that, I packed clothes, including pants and my favourite hoodie dress and shoes including high heeled boots and sandals. I needed to prepare for the rain so I also packed a full set of waterproofs. Lastly, I wandered into my bedroom and said "Bye Bye" and got my teddy. As you can see, I got a bit carried away and half emptied my house!

Chapter Three: On The Drive - Stopping Off For Snacks

I was in the car and it was the BIG day! I was on the way to the jungle. After an hour to two, I stopped off for some snacks. I had a fruit and fibre snack bar and two pieces of toast with peanut butter and jam (pre-cooked at my house) followed by a crunchy apple and a refreshing bunch of grapes. And for good measure, I threw in a delicious chocolate chip biscuit. For my drink I had a raspberry tonic water.

Chapter Four: Calling To Look After My Pets

Whilst my car was being charged, I decided to make a few calls to check the arrangements I had put in place to look after my pets were all working out ok.

I phoned my Mum first to see how Ava the armadillo was getting on. Then I checked on Freddie the fox who was being looked after by my Dad.

They both said it was going smoothly, but Ava the armadillo had done a wee on the floor. Oops!

Chapter Five: First Day In The Jungle

After a long car journey, Brian and I arrived at our destination. Then we saw a statue of the Queen. It looked funny though. Then it started moving and we realised IT WAS THE QUEEN!

Chapter Six: The Steal

We had a chat with the Queen and all planned to go and steal the famous Jungle Crown and Royal Coconut. The Queen had wanted them for a long time but nobody had managed to find them and bring them back successfully.

We went deep into the jungle, found some locked boxes and had to complete a number puzzle to unlock them and release the Jungle Crown and Royal Coconut. WE DID IT! And we all jumped for joy. But once the find had sunk in I realised that something didn't feel quite right. But I pushed the thought out of my mind because everyone else seemed so happy.

Chapter Seven: The Chat

After a night's sleep, Brian and I met up and we weren't very happy about stealing from the jungle, even if it was for the Queen. So we decided to have a chat with her. I was secretly hoping that we would decide to put the Crown and Coconut back in the jungle where they belong and that we could go home. I was missing home.

We had a chat and decided to return the treasure tomorrow. We built a den and a camp fire to stay overnight ready to return our loot in the morning. The den wasn't water-tight. Good thing I packed a full set of waterproofs!

Chapter Eight: Putting Back What Isn't Ours

We walked past a gushing blue stream and we even saw five frogs hopping near the trees! The jungle was full of wildlife. But we had to stay focused on our mission. Me and Brian were getting tired so we hurried along, returned the treasure and retraced our steps. We got back to the den and collected our things. We hopped in our car and drove away.

Chapter Nine: Home

When I got home, I read a book and went to sleep. The next morning, I played Monopoly, Scrabble and Patience. You might be wondering with who… Well guess what? My new boyfriend, Brian. Although it was fun and a true adventure we learned an important lesson in the jungle.

We learned that even though the Crown and Coconut were truly magnificent, and even though the Queen is really special, it was wrong to steal them from the jungle.

We did the right thing to put them back where they belonged, however glorious they were.

Once upon a Plane

By D. Walton

Once Upon a Time the world's biggest passenger plane also known as the Airbus A380. The plane was set to fly from Dublin to Florida, a 24 hour flight.

With 500 passengers on business class and 500 passengers on first class, in total the plane was holding 1,000 passengers. 12 hours into the flight the plane crashed into the Atlantic ocean from 2000 feet in the air. 998 people died and 2 people survived.

Security!

By David Johnson

It all started at night in the city. The raid was in an exotic house full of security systems including a cactus room in there to stop them.

"Okay," he said. "We shall go in there and steal, then we escape before the cops show up."

They were in there but not for long the alarms start ringing.

"HEY, FREEZE!" yelled the cops.

"It's the fuzz!" they said and then they got hit by some cactuses. They were captured!

"We can't thank you enough," the guys said. "If you hadn't delayed those robbers we might never would've caught them last night."

"Well I'm always be there to help, take care officer! See you," he said and he waved.

The One and Only

By Ethan Ogle

One day, Edward the blue engine was waiting at Wellsworth with a passenger train.

"How much longer driver?" Asked Edward.

"Well, in five minutes old boy," said his driver.

Just then, there was a loud *bang!* In the distance. It was the powerplant at Brendam.

"Gosh darn it!" said Charlie. "I knew this would happen!"

"Everyone get in quickly!" yelled Edward.

Everyone cleared the platform faster than they ever had before.

"Full speed ahead, Edward!" exclaimed Charlie frantically, as he blew the whistle and Edward was off and away.

They soon saw Donald heading the other way, pulling 2 slow goods.

"Donald, run!" yelled Edward as he rushed past.

"Oh, no!" said Donald as he screeched his brakes on and closed his eyes as the shockwave struck him.

"Come on, Edward, Faster!" yelled Sydney, who was his fireman.

"I'm going as fast as I can!" he replied, pushing himself to his limits.

They shot through Crosby and that was when the shockwave struck!

Just then, there was a clang! As Edward's front pony truck wheels derailed on a set of points.

"Flipping godred sake!" said Edward, but his wheels got back on the track and soon they saw it.

"Knapford, dead ahead!" exclaimed Charlie.

They arrived in Knapford and everyone was hurried into the station buildings.

"Phew, we made it," said Edward, glad to have escaped the Brendam bay blast.

After they heard the cause of the blast on the radio, they heard a whistle.

"James?" exclaimed Edward, as he saw James pull in looking very cross. "Are you okay, James?" Edward asked him.

"No, Edward, I'm not okay at all!" James said angrily.

Judging by how he reacted, James had definitely seen something that the rest of them hadn't seen.

"Weesh, James! Why are you so angry?" asked Edward, wondering what was going on with him.

"Well, one, the powerplant blew up, and two, I left half of my train behind because Toby went to get Henrietta from Crovan's Gate works," said James, finishing his sentence in a fiery tone.

"Oh, James, I'm so sorry," said Edward.

"No, Edward. I'm really angry at the moment. Anyways, I was going to head to the Vicarstown Bridge to get to the mainland, are you coming with me?" asked James.

"Well, I was going to see if any one else... James? ...James!!" said Edward who then noticed James was puffing away to the mainland.

The next day, Edward's crew decided it best to head to the Vicarstown Bridge and along the way they stopped at Wellswort so they could give Edward a drink of water.

Just then, they heard James' whistle as he shot past hoping to get to the bridge.

Just at that moment, Edward realised that the points were set towards Suddery.

"James!! You're heading towards Suddery," yelled Edward, but it was too late.

James began to cough and feel pain in his face and that's when it happened. James was mutated!

"AAAAHHH!" James screamed. Just then, he crashed off the rails!

Meanwhile, at Wellsworth, Edward and Sydney were waiting for Charlie to come back with news of survivors. But soon his two way radio started to make static.

It was Jem Cole, Trevor's owner. He said "I survived, along with my wife and daughter in a bunker in the house, however the same couldn't be said for Trevor, the blast got him bad.

"I had my rifle on me and I put the traction engine out of his misery," finished Jem.

Charlie told Edward about Trevor and he broke down in tears when he was told about Trevor.

"God, I hope this nightmare ends soon," said Charlie.

"I hope it will end soon as well," said Edward.

The next day, they woke up to rain pelting down on Edward's cab roof and he was low on his coal capacity, then they heard a whistle.

It was Percy who was pulling Annie, Clarabel and S. C. Ruffey on the back. They didn't stop to check on them.

They decided to check the Killdane Ironworks for any survivors.

Sadly, no-one was there. The only thing which remained was the hollowed out corpse of another engine whose shape was all too familiar.

"oh… my… god," exclaimed Edward after seeing a horrible sight in front of him.

There was only one great western pannier tank on the island, and they knew that they had lost Duck.

He had no eyes and a gaping hole in his forehead, just looking at the sight of him made Charlie want to vomit.

Several pieces had been ripped off of him, he was missing a siderod and a few sections of handrail. To add to that, it seemed as if the whole engine was completely hollow. Boiler tubes, water tanks and bunker all empty, even the ashes at the bottom of his firebox were gone.

"I'm so sorry, Duck. We were too late," said Edward, saddened by the loss of the NWR's No. 8 Engine.

They decided to leave and while doing so, spotted Arry and Bert, the Ironworks twins. They were just empty shells, tossed aside off the line. They didn't stick around for long.

They began heading down the line to Killdane and they couldn't believe what they saw.

It was Henry, Gordon and a bunch of workmen, as safe as can be in a goods shed. The two engines were glad to see him again, but seemed to be a bit focused on something else.

They had travelled down the line to see if anyone needs help, but stopped two days ago when trying to reach the ironworks.

An engine was blocking their path.

"Hey, can you move please?" asked the two engines, but suddenly, the engine charged at them and started to make unsettling loud roars.

Henry and Gordon were frightened and charged back down to Killdane with the engine stopping.

Apparently, several engines had stopped by here recently.

Henry and Gordon noticed Percy pass by yesterday morning and the night before. D261 shot past, he didn't say anything, but all Henry and Gordon could hear was him trying to scream.

"We lost Frederick the other night, the blasted engine had gone after him. He thought that he was a safe distance from the tracks. How wrong he was," said Henry, telling Edward what had happened to Frederick.

The next day the three Railway engines were out on the line, when they saw Percy, who was derailed in a ditch. His jaw was broken and dislocated. Charlie couldn't look at it. He felt like he was going to be sick.

No one wanted to put him out of his misery, so they just decided to leave him there.

Edward picked up Annie, Clarabel and Scruffey from the back and said sadly "Percy… I'm sorry…" with tears falling from his eyes.

They didn't dare to look back, because they'd only feel more guilty for leaving Percy in the ditch.

They arrived back at Killdane where Scruffey began thinking of a battle plan. They were going to use him as bait for Oliver, but he had brake troubles, so this interrupted their strategy.

Soon after, Skarloey's driver called on two way radio and told him the depressing story of what happened to the narrow gauge no.1.

He said "Skarloey got mutated by the radiation, but he said that the passengers on his train needed him, so we kept going."

His driver paused for a moment and said "When we got to Crovan's Gate where Rheneas and Duncan were sitting, they were in shock when they saw Skarloey, he was horribly mutated. I pointed my gun at his head and said 'I'm sorry' as I pulled the trigger." Finishing his sentence sadly.

The next day, Edward, Henry and Gordan woke up to find that Scruffey was gone and also, Paul and Garret have gone missing too.

Edward headed back to Tidmouth and near the sheds they saw Leonard. He told them he was ill and stayed home on the 4th, good he did. Otherwise who knows what would have happened to him.

They stopped at Tidmouth sheds and Leonard fainted at the sight that awaited him… it was Thomas. He was horribly mutated but other than that he was almost the same engine that we knew and loved.

He told them what happened to him during the blast, apparently Thomas was shunting trucks at Knapford Station when the blast occurred.

Werewolves

By Jack B

School was going on a field trip to old castle and an old village with stories about werewolves attacking the old village in the 1500s when there was a full moon.

The school came from Sunderland. The teacher met an old man wearing old clothing. The old man was weird and smelled like a wet dog. One of the students looked at his eyes which were yellow like a wolf's!

The student and the teacher learn that the old man was smart and now it was nighttime and there was a full moon.

The teacher tells them to run as some werewolves show up and the old man turned into a werewolf himself and attack the teacher and student when the sun rise!

It was too late!

The Man with no Face!

By Anonymous

On an ordinary day, a girl called Lily-May was in her bedroom when all of a sudden she heard chains getting dragged along the grass inn the back garden. She looked out the window and seen a man staring up at her. The weird thing is he didn't have a face!

He had a bag with chains wrapped around his face and he was holding an AXE in his hand.

She shouted for her sister. Her sister came running in and looked out the window. She could also see the man so the sister ran downstairs, locked all the doors and closed all the windows and ran back upstairs. She couldn't see the man anymore, but Lily-May could.

There were also lambs in the back garden and got their head chopped off with the axe.

The 2 sisters couldn't see the man anymore so they went outside and their dad just got back from work to see his two girls dead on the floor and out of nowhere he seen the man running towards him!

The man killed the two girls, the baby lambs and the dad, then put the baby lambs in a hole he had made, and put the two girls and dad in a big tree to hide the evidence.

But will he be back for more people? I guess we will never know…!

The Boy and his Dog

By Ashton Heskett

A boy called Fin woke up with his dog next to him. Fin loved his dog Rex so much, he went everywhere with him.

Fin got ready to walk his dog. Fin packed a bag of treats, water, ball, dog poo bags. He set off. Fin went to a field to play ball with Rex, Fin flinged the ball as hard as he could then Rex ran as fast as he could at the ball while barking cheerfully.

But then a man runs at Rex and picks him up and runs off but Fin turns into a lion and pounced at the man and mauls him!

He runs off screaming for help.

Fin got his dog back, he bombarded the dog with treats making sure Rex is okay.

The Boy who Lived!

By Logan Lamb

The boy Harry was excited because he got a pet owl for his birthday. He called it Hedwig, a big guy called Hagrid got it for him. Harry was strict because he wanted to go away.

Harry was angry because his grandparents was strict. Harry went on the Hogwards express on his way to school. Harry made some friends. Harry kept on hearing voices in his head. Harry thinks it's the man who killed his parents.

Harry was in a strict Quilitch mach. Grifindors, Slivine and Harry got the golden snitch. Grifindor won and everyone cheered.

The End

The Party

By Robbie Adey

Dan has invited Max, Marshall, Peter, Dan, Sam and Katie to his massive beautiful mansion living with Katie (Sam's wife).

Then they came, when they do the lights flicker. Then Dan is gone!

They gasp, only blood and guts were seen on the floor. Sam and Max were scanning the kitchen to see a suspicious book.

Max says "tell me your secrets."

Sam added on, "just read it."

Max replied "it doesn't have pictures."

When Sam wasn't looking Max died, then the people saw that Katie did it, so she went into lava.

the end

The Explosion

By Max Lishman

A boy named Micale was getting ready for school. His dad was always out, so his big sister was always doing the work for him. The bus came and said goodbye to his sister.

She sat down and watched TV. The news said that some power plants were down.

Micale was in the bus with his friends, Joseph and Shawn and Alfie. There was a kid who was on his games all the time. They went to school, the teacher said school will be closed early.

The kids were confused about that.

Later on the news said one power plant was still on. The workers said the power is too high and Micale and his sister's dad was there. Then it exploded, a huge wave went global. Micale and his sister were at the hospital then people were turning into characters. Everyone was shocked, there were destruction everywhere.

The gamer was destroying everything!

The kids fight back, but he was powerful. Micale and his sister and friends went back to the power plant to fix it but the gamer was there. They got him and fix the world.

Robot Attack!

By Arthur, Oscar, Henry, James, Bonallie

A long time ago there was a boy with his dad and they were mechanics living in a scrap yard and they were working on an old car called Bessy and the dad told his son to go and get some more parts for the car. He went out to the usual pile of parts ad he found a massive part what looks tto be a massive thumb.

He went to the warehouse. His dad tells him not to go in there but he decided to go in there anyways and found something insane. A massive robot,, it looks like it was powered down so the boy kicks the massive robot and it turned on.

The boy was terrified and he ran back to the garage and told his dad.

His dad did not believe him, he said "bull sh?#!"

The massive robot rips open the roof and magically fixed Bessy, and the dad said "No f~#?ing way!"

The dad was so confused and said to the boy "you weren't lying were you? This is insane!"

The dad also said "We need to tell the government!"

The boy said "no because they will destroy him!"

"Okay," the dad said. "We'll not tell the government."

2 weeks later

"Hey dad, I'm going to go and check on the robot!"

"Okay, be careful!"

"Okay, dad!"

The boy went to the warehouse to find it empty.

"Oh sh###!! Dad, dad!!"

"What, son?"

"The robot is missing!"

"Are you joking?"

"No dad, I'm deadly serious."

"He could not have got far."

Later in the city on the radio it said "a massive robot taking the city!"

The father and son duo sped down. The 3 attack helicopters surround the massive robot.

The father and son duo drive through the barricades and head straight to the robot and luckily the robot notices the father and son duo driving towards them. He picks them up and the father and son duo say "he is friendly! He is just scared of the helicopters!"

The government tells the pilots to land. When they land the robot waves to the pilots.

6 months later the robot made news and he is part of Jericho city and he helps fix cars and move heavy things.

THE END

Yeeeesss!

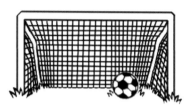

By Harry G

It was a cold rainy day at the Stadium of Light, Sunderland. We're hoping for hope to survive in the league, there was attendance of 40,000 fans at the Stadium, chants were coming from the home and the away end. It just hit 3 PM and the Lads come out with the BPA squad.

Both captains, Hannah Ebbie-White and Bobby Kerr stepped up. "BPA get kick-off!" says the referee.

Hannah kicks the ball to Sophie, they're off, BPA were on the attack, Ebbie-White to Williams. She shoots.

Yeeeees!

BPA have scored, 1-0.

What are Sunderland doing? Really bad defending from Ballard and Cirkin. Sunderland send the ball down the field, Andy tries to stop Kevin Ball but Ball worked his magic, he chipped the ball over Lynn Conway's head. Yeeeees! Kevin Ball has equalised for Sunderland 1-1. The home crowd goes wild. Sophie says "we can't let them win, come on girls we can do this."

BPA gets it underway yet again. Rebecca passes to Sophie, to Hannah, Ebbie-White shoots, what a save by Patterson. Goes to Kerr, to Amad, to Ball to Quinn.

Yesssssssss!

2-1 Sunderland.

"Just before half time, you have got to be kidding!" Says Rosie.

Sunderland are 2-1 in front.

Substitute for Sunderland, coming off is number 28, Jermain Defoe and coming on is number 9, Kevin Phillips. Phillips comes on to get Sunderland the win, come on lads.

It's now the second half and 52 minutes into the match, still 2-1 to Sunderland. Phillips to Amad, to Cattermole, to Kerr. Oh no! He has hit the bar. Dear oh dear.

Substitute for Sunderland, coming off is Dennis Cirkin and coming on is Mark McNicol.

Jodie to Rosie, Rosie runs down the wing, she shoots.

Yeeees!

I can't believe it, it's 2-2, Rosie has scored past Sunderland.

It's all gone wrong for Sunderland, it's 2-2, 55 minutes gone. What's going on here, Rosie has done a cartwheel into the Sunderland end. The Lads are livid!

Ball to McNicol, to Amad. What a challenge by Holly, she runs with the ball, 59 minutes in, Mark slides in. Oh dear, there is an injury for BPA. Holly is down injured. I think she has broken her leg. Mark McNicol is in some trouble. BPA back room staff come to remove Holly from the pitch. The ref is having a word with Mark, he's off, Mark is shown a red card, 72 minutes in Sunderland are down to 10 men.

BPA get underway, Rosie to Sophie, Rebecca to Glen, he strikes. Ohh - just hit the post!! Patterson gives it to Quinn, to Phillips on the volley.

Oh My Word! Absolutely sensational. Kevin Phillips scores his 10th goal this season to give Sunderland a 3-2 lead. Ebbie-White shakes her head with disappointment.

Can the Lads survive? We get it underway, BPA are on the attack. Sunderland intercept, Kerr to Amad, to Kerr. Yeeeeeeees! Sunderland stay in the Premier League. 4-2. Brilliant! BPA are out of the league, the Stadium of Light rise up. It ends Sunderland 4 – BPA 2.

About the Team

Simon Berry

Simon has been an Optometrist for over 20 years. He opened his own community Optometry Practice in 2002.

He gets bored quickly and has lots of little projects to keep life more interesting. One of the ones he is most proud of is the Gilesgate Story Challenge.

He is passionate about books and when flirting with a different career he did try and write a few himself. (None were ever published.) He had a literary agent for a while but they left soon after to become a coffee barista and he lost his contract. He hopes this wasn't because of having him as a client.

Contact Simon at:
simon@simonberry.co.uk

Or visit the Practice website:
www.simonberry.co.uk

Lisette Auton

Lisette Auton's work focuses on identity, process, kindness and access. Disabled, neurodivergent and northern, some say she's a word artist, she says she does stuff with words. As a writer and artist she works with words in all their forms: as an author and playwright, a film and theatre maker, as a solo artist, with collaborators, and alongside wonderful humans as a creative practitioner and mentor.

Lisette is an award-winning poet; the 2019 Early Careers Fellow for Literature at Cove Park; on the TSS Publishing list of Best British & Irish Flash Fiction; and winner of The Journal Culture Award 2021 for Performance of the Year for *Writing the Missing – A River Cycle* commissioned by Durham Book Festival. Her debut middle grade novel *The Secret of Haven Point* was published by Puffin in February 2022, and *The Stickleback Catchers* in February 2023.

You'll find Lisette's work in galleries, online, in theatres and bookshops, as well as random places such as laundrettes and railway station waiting rooms.

Find out More:

https://lisetteauton.co.uk/

Kylie Dixon

Kylie Dixon is an artist and illustrator living in the North East of England. After 18 years of working in a bank, she walked away and decided to follow her dream of making a living from creating beautiful things. Her obsession with mushrooms began as she pondered her next artistic move whilst walking through the woods. Looking down at her feet, Kylie noticed an abundance of tiny mushrooms. Giving it a 'goog', she read that spotting mushrooms in the wild was a symbol of positivity, and so her art business 'Mushroom Marvellous' was born. Every piece of artwork created had a hand-illustrated mushroom in the design, as a gesture of hope and positive change.

From there, and with the encouragement of her 'shroomy' followers , Kylie's first foray into her authory life began. Kylie now has three books and a colouring book all taking place in The Magical World of Mushroom Marvellous. These stories, based upon real life action in her Dad's allotment, are now inspiring children all over the North East – and wider – to believe in themselves.

Find out More:

https://magicalworldofmushroommarvellous.com/

Sam Strong

Sam is a freelance illustrator and full-time lecturer at Aston University where she teaches optics to optometry students. Her most exciting achievement to date is that she's written and illustrated her own textbook titled "Introduction to Visual Optics: A Light Approach".

One of her biggest passions in life is combining her love of science and illustration to help make tricky topics accessible to as many people as possible.

Her second passion in life is cat videos.

Contact Sam:

s.strong2@aston.ac.uk

Or follow her on Twitter:

@samanthastrong

Miles Nelson

Miles is an independent author, illustrator, and bookshop owner from Durham. Whilst he loves to tell stories of his own, his favourite thing in the world is to help and inspire young writers to hone their skills.

Miles specializes in young adult and children's fantasy, although he has a special soft spot for nature writing. His bestselling debut, *Riftmaster*, was released in 2021. It tells the story of a college student who is whisked away from Earth by a mysterious force called the Rift, and encourages readers to find joy in the unknown. Renegade, its much-anticipated sequel, is out now!

He also runs the independent LGBTQ+ book shop, BookWyrm Durham, alongside his husband, Chris.

Contact Miles:

milesnelson1997@outlook.com

milesnelsonofficial.com

@Probablymiles on Twitter

Contact BookWyrm:

BookWyrm.co.uk

@BookWyrmDurham on Instagram, Twitter and Facebook

Esther Robson

Still retired, still enjoying reading and still loving the Gilesgate Story Challenge! It's great to see the authors developing their style and writing with such confidence.

It's been great fun reading this year's entries. I'm astounded by the imagination of the children and can't wait to read the winning story to my little grandson, Bunny!

Hoping for many more to come!

About the Cause

The Toby Henderson Trust is an independently funded charity supporting autistic children, young people and adults, their families and carers in the North East of England. We provide relevant, appropriate and accessible support for autistic young people from two years into adulthood, whilst also empowering parents, families and carers by sharing knowledge, experience and understanding.

We initially opened the door to our first site at The Old Barn in 2001 with only our founder, Lesley, a telephone, and a passion to make a difference. And now over 20 years later, we have supported hundreds and thousands of families. Our work remains crucial to so many and gives us huge satisfaction and joy.

Thank you to every one of you who have purchased this book to help us raise much needed funds to continue our amazing work with autistic children, young people and adults in the North East.

Guest Illustrators

Aside from our lead illustrator, Sam, we had several wonderful illustrators involved from new college. These illustrators contributed some incredible work with a huge variety and bold style.

- **Aeron Irwin** – The Lumberjack Horror Story
- **Bonnie-Blue Mongan** – The Unexpected Visitor, The Lumberjack Horror Story
- **Cait Stott** – The Mystery of Goldsmith Manor title page
- **Elliot Conway** – The Unexpected Visitor Comic
- **Finlay R** – The Laboratory
- **Izzy Reed** – The Laboratory Comic
- **Jaymie-Leigh Hall** – Christopher's Biscuit adventure, All Hail the Caesar, Doors, The Unexpected Visitor title page, The Adventures of Donald the Fish
- **Jessica Orr** – The Adventures of Donald the Fish
- **Kate Loughran** – Karen's Catastrophe Title Page
- **Kayleigh-Marie Hume** – The Clown who Drowned
- **Mollie Thompson** – Christopher's Biscuit Adventure title page
- **Nathan Rose** – The Laboratory Title Page
- **Owen Young** – The Mystery of Goldsmith Manor
- **Sophie Hughes** – Christopher's Biscuit Adventure
- **Victoria Moralee** – The Adventures of Donald the Fish

Help us grow...

We need your help for our competition to become bigger and better each year.

Search for us online:

www.TheGilesgateStoryChallenge.com

Like us on Facebook and Instagram:

@gilesgatestorychallenge

Share our tweets:

@gilesgatestory1

But mostly - tell all your friends to buy the book!